A STRANDED id

PROLOGUE

I remember everything. Every time I close my eyes, memories come rushing back, taking me back to a place and time when agony and despair were the only real emotions to guide me. The clarity of my thoughts and nightmares haunt me, and I have accepted the fact that these memories will never go away. This battering ram of pain knocked down my interior walls of morality a long time ago, only it did not retreat when the fight was over, when I gave up. Time really does *fly* by with age, once you get past a certain point, though I have no idea when that particular point is. And I hear people say this all the time, but it truly does seem like it all happened yesterday. Of course it all began years ago, when I was merely a boy. I was a jovial two years old, not quite potty trained, and constantly left in shit.

The nightmares began on a Fourth of July, and this is important to note because in an instant, my life changed that day, I changed.

In front of family and friends, my father walked out and never came back. My mother never drank until that night, and never drank again until the next Fourth of July. That's when she thought about the *slut* that took my father away. This cycle continued for years, and even though I wished and prayed for her to stop, she never did. I wanted to believe that she did not know what she was doing to me. Even grasped at thinking she did not mean to, that she just could not hear me when I begged her to stop. In the end, I think she was simply numb to the cold pool of wetness my tears left behind every time my innocence was taken from me.

It really didn't matter what I believed, I was always wrong.

So I just stopped believing in everything.

It was easier that way, easier to deal with her!

But not only did I stop believing in everything, I made a choice not to care about anything anymore either. For me, there was no right or wrong, no heaven or hell, and happiness was certainly far from my horizon of worry.

The only thing I was sure of is that once a year another July would come. Albeit uninvited, it inevitably came, right after June damn it, right after the asphalt turned scorching hot when high temperatures and long summer days moved into the area. I was used to the heat and humidity, but I hated it. My everyday sweat constantly reminded me of my tears. Only my tears were icy cold, like death, while my sweat was steaming hot, like the anger I felt boiling inside me.

That anger I knew I'd eventually exploit. I felt it growing inside me, changing me, much like puberty, but my voice never cracked and I never relented. I was turning into a man, an angry man, with no beliefs, cares, or worries to cling to.

That made me dangerous, very dangerous, but

I still had a ways to go.

And then another Fourth of July came. The last of the sunshine disappeared around nine o'clock that night. It was like that every summer night in the south, but I stayed awake anyway, hoping something would happen, a miracle, so it could remain July 3rd forever. Impossible, I knew, so I came up with more plausible scenarios. I wished a tree would fall on the house, wanted aliens to abduct me. I'd rather them touch me than my mom anyway. And I lived at the beach, so I even wished for a tidal wave to come and wash my worries away, wash *everything* away.

And then I got up the next morning, and knew none of my wishes had come true because I had to do just that, *get up*! It was no surprise, really, I had been unlucky my entire life. Wait a minute. Is that what I'm calling my existence, *a life?*

Dad would say "beggars can't be choosers," and he was right.

My mom and I *begged* him to stay, but he *chose* to leave anyway.

I *begged* my mom to stop hurting me, to stop drinking, but ya know what, she *chose* to do shit to me anyway.

I thought about running away that morning, after I mowed the grass and started sweating drops of anger and death. But I changed my mind when my aunt, uncle and two cousins arrived. My cousins are younger than I, and not from the beach, so I knew they looked up to me, and wanted to learn all the things I'd gotten good at over the years, like surfing and fishing. But guess what, I did not care…at all.

Sure, I escorted them to the beach while the grownups got reacquainted back at the house. The surf and sand was within walking distance, but to be honest, if one of my young, city slicker cousins were to have started drowning or panicking after slurping down mouthfuls of bitter Atlantic saltwater, I would not have tried to save them.

That did not happen, but if it did, I'm sure I would not have cared.

No one ever came to help me when I screamed.

I would have probably smiled because I knew the sound of crashing waves would eventually muffle their cries for help.

And I know what you are thinking but I'm merely being honest.

I would have watched them die.

I would have watched death consume them, the same way it was slowly, methodically consuming me.

Dinner was good though, mom always cooked well. That night consisted of grilled hamburgers and hotdogs, baked beans and potato salad, an American tradition for the Fourth of July I think. The patties were pressed with chopped onions and green peppers, and a dry packet of ranch dressing mix. Everyone loved the burgers. My mother was a genius when it came to adding ingredients to an already perfected recipe, and I do not cook often, but on the occasion that I do grill hamburgers, I still make them the same way. I can't help it. Those damn hamburgers were good.

Still, that night, mom was drinking again, but no one thought anything of it except me.

In fact, throughout the whole meal, I eyeballed her Vodka drink the same way I eyeballed my dad's collection of dirty magazines he must have forgotten about. He had left them in the garage, hidden inside the lawn mower bag he never used. "It's always better to mulch," he used to say. "Good fertilizer for the grass. Keeps sod greener longer." Yeah right, although that might actually be true, in my father's case, it was complete bullshit.

He was just hiding his collection of *tits* and *ass* from mom.

I hid them from her too. Only, I hid them in my room, behind my chest of drawers because when I touch myself I like to be comfortable and private. I did it out in the shed, a few times, but I felt eyes draped all over me, like the flannel bathrobe I knew my mom would be wearing when she came for me later on that night.

Yep, it was just another typical Fourth of July. Isn't life grand?

I remember everyone filtering into the backyard to watch the crafty, booming fireworks show as my mother poured yet another drink. I could smell the pineapple and orange juice, but mostly Vodka as she walked behind me to join the others outside. Then, without saying a word, she ran her long fingers through my hair, and at that moment I knew something was different about that night, about me.

I promised myself things would be different. It was time for a change.

It was time to write my own story.

And while everyone was in the backyard and in awe of the brilliant lights that brought a thunderous roar to what was otherwise a crystal clear, picture perfect coastal night, I escaped into my bedroom, left the door open, retrieved my father's, I mean my stash of filthy magazines, and began doing filthy things to myself.

This might shock you, but I've you told this already.

I just don't care about anything anymore.

Someone should have saved me a long time ago.

1

July 3rd.

Brilliance and paranoia consumed Abraham Kinsinger like the high of a crack addict.

The itch was back, he knew because he sensed eyes watching his every move, a different shadow around every corner. But no one could see him, no one ever saw him. Still, this time of year he always needed reassurance, needed to know everything was okay. His plan was not perfect, but there was always room to improvise, he knew, and always a chance he would get caught. Not likely, he mused, but he had to consider the possibility, it helped him focus, helped him limit mistakes.

The itch always came and went, left him alone for a while, but always came back, like clockwork when it was time to hunt again. Every year brought with it a new hunting season.

And he loved to hunt!

The animalistic itch, the fever, always started consuming him the beginning of May. He'd been able to hold off the urge to kill for a while, but six years ago things changed, changed for good, when he decided to feed the itch.

And it shocked him at how easy, delightful it was.

Still was, every year after that.

Only he was better at it now, more skilled, efficient, better prepared than ever before.

And he knew his hunting grounds well.

Born and raised in St. Augustine, Florida, the coastal community was the only home Abraham knew, and he watched people flock to America's oldest established city to celebrate the Fourth of July every year. He'd watch them fall victim to the many tourist traps outlining San Marco Ave. The one he hated the most was the Fountain of Youth.

Abraham had grown up just over the bridge on Vilano Beach, a smaller, more discreet portion of the old city, and unbeknownst to the tourists that wallowed to St. Augustine. However, the locals knew it well, especially the bar scene. And before he began hunting, he used to frequent the bars as well, meet the perfect girl, get her drunk, and take her home to do filthy things to her, imitating what he saw in his dirty magazines.

Those women were never hard to meet. He was 5'10", weighed a meaningful 185 lbs, and his skin was golden, bronzed to perfection by the sun. Abraham's good looks were always noticed. His dirty blonde hair complimented his ocean-blue eyes, and he kept his face, legs, chest, and arms clean-shaven.

He hated hair.

He hated anything that might get in the way of his hunting.

He even tried going bald once, but noticed an immediate change in his stature with women. With a head that glistened in the sun, they found him less attractive, so he waited for his hair to return. It took nearly four months for the length to return to the way it was when he was getting laid. That was the longest 124 days of his life, and a blistering time period for the palms of his hands.

He knew the hair on his head might threaten his freedom one day, thanks to DNA, but Abraham had trained his mind to think clearly long ago. He processed things quickly, quicker than most, and his paranoid nature helped limit mistakes. He could not afford to make any. He was exceptionally hard on himself.

Nevertheless, every time a girl came home with him from the bars, getting excited proved difficult. No matter what she did to him, no matter how warm he felt inside her mouth, the excitement, the adrenaline rush was never there. Unless, the girl liked it rough. He cherished the memories of those women who wanted to be roughed up. Some would beg for it, wanting to be hit, and every time a memory came of a girl who wanted him to choke them, no matter where he was or what he was doing, an erection sprouted and would not retreat until he took matters into his own hands.

And that's when he first noticed the itch inside him.

The hunger...craving...for infinite control hung over him like a raincloud.

But he was able to control it for a while. Throughout most of his twenties, getting laid on Vilano Beach proved easy. It was just off A1A, the forever popular beachfront avenue, and the beach itself was one of the few in the state of Florida that allowed people to drive on it. An old drawbridge, which was in the process of being replaced by a new waterway, also connected Vilano with San Marco Avenue, which led to the always-busy, touristy St. George St.

St. George St. was the hotspot of St. Augustine this time of year, directly across from the Old Fort, one of the landmarks of the old Spanish settlement. All of the restaurants, shops, bars, and galleries stayed open late, to house the drunks, and accommodate the big spenders.

And St. George St. is where Abraham started hunting six years ago.

The itch was really strong now, more potent

than ever before. But it was only July 3rd.... one more day to go, *no exceptions. Just wait,* he told himself. *That's all you have to do.* Someone would come to him, they always did, and even though he toyed with the notion of hunting early, strongly believed he'd get away with it, he chose to stick to the plan. He was meticulous, neat, and patient. He knew the big Fourth of July crowd and the boisterous roar of the fireworks would mask what he was doing. It would be too easy for someone to detect him today, not worth it. He had put a lot of work into this, planning began back in May, when he scouted the area like a hawk, all in preparation for this particular weekend.

No exceptions, there was a reason the Fourth of July was circled in red ink on his calendar every year.

He could not risk getting caught, and would not go home empty handed. *It's too risky.* He spoke to himself a lot. *Stick with the plan. Be patient. You don't want to wind up in prison, like all the others, waiting to die.*

"Fuck it," he said aloud. He smoked, threw his cigarette butt on the ground, put it out with a quick twist of his boot heel, then leaned over, picked it up and carried it inside the hotel room on the bottom floor of the Ramada Inn on San Marco Avenue. He put the butt with all the others in the zip-lock bag on the dresser. When the time came he would not leave anything behind. He even wanted to quit smoking, but trying to fight that urge proved about as useless as fighting the itch inside him. So, he had to be careful.

And he was.

When he arrived at the hotel earlier that afternoon, he paid for the room with cash. He used cash for everything, though a stolen credit card was used to reserve the room. He stayed in the same room back in May, requested it, used a fake name, and provided the license plate number of his car, although that particular tag he'd stolen off the back of a Jeep Cherokee in a McDonald's parking lot one block over on Ponce De Leon Blvd.

"Thank you Mr. Cundy," the Spanish receptionist could barely speak English, and never made eye contact. This was good, because it allowed him to check out the security monitors behind the counter to see if anything had changed since his May visit.

It had not.

His room was still the only one not intruded upon by the spying lenses of security cameras.

Still, the other cameras were recording.

He did not like that.

But it was only the 3rd, he reminded himself.

He could take care of the security cameras tomorrow.

Now, as he sat on the bed of the hotel room, the itch began to creep down his spine and seep into his loins. He started remembering his first victim, then the second, third, fourth, and fifth. He had an orgasm before he even got hard and had his shaft in his hands.

"Yep," Abraham said aloud as he turned on the local news. "I can take care of the security cameras tomorrow. I can take care of everything tomorrow!" And then he smiled, and zipped up his pants.

A news anchor was in the middle of warning the young women in St. Augustine to use good judgment and to not talk to strangers or go anywhere alone. He was sure the newscaster made these statements in reference to him, because of what he had done the past five years. But Abraham also knew none of that mattered.

Someone would not listen.

Someone was always alone.

And someone always enjoyed meeting a good-looking stranger.

Someone always did…always.

And just that quickly, the itch returned.

*

Ernest Paul Kidder had all the connections, but on the brink nonetheless, and his battle with stress had been a one-sided fight thus far. He had thrown in the towel long ago, but the beating continued, mercilessly, with no end in sight. It came with the job, he knew, and he had asked for it, had worked hard to climb within the ranks, although most felt sure his father had pulled some strings. He had not, of course, but people were going to think that anyway. He did not care, and didn't have enough time to spar with rumors. He would probably get his ass kicked anyway, just like with the stress, and the stranglehold it had on him. Still, no matter what people thought, like it or not, he was the youngest senior detective the St. John's County Sheriff's Department had ever honored. And Kidder took his job very seriously, the respect he did have was earned.

Now, however, his stomach tightened with a nauseating sickness that made his knees buckle. He watched darkness fall over St. Augustine, knew another sunrise was sure to follow, and with it meant another Fourth of July would hypnotize St. John's County. Everyone knew a killer was prowling the humid streets of St. Augustine this time every year, but there were no leads, no suspects, and no useful evidence of any kind.

More importantly, there was no way to stop *him.*

The local newspaper, *The St. Augustine Record*, held off a media firestorm by keeping the term *serial killer* out of the headlines and he was genuinely thankful for that. The city could not afford an absence of tourists this time of year. Millions were brought into this quaint, coastal community every July. Also, the Editor in Chief had landed his position at the paper largely due to the influence of the Kidder family name. His father must have called in a favor, he was sure. It seemed like everyone owed his father something.

Still, consecutively for the past five years, every Fourth of July, a girl has gone missing, disappearing without a trace.

Two bodies were recovered later, the brutality revealed by what was left of flesh and bone.

And three girls were still missing, but Kidder suspected their fate had reached the same tragic end.

Now EP, his nickname throughout the department and the town, sat behind his desk sipping on a cold, obtrusive stale cup of coffee. He was sure another unknowing young woman would wake up tomorrow for the final time in her life. The party scene was alive in St. Augustine this time of year. Alcohol did not help the Sheriff's Office in their investigation and resources were often wasted on irrelevant 911 calls or unnecessary domestic disturbances.

He knew the killer liked, perhaps even thrived on the commotion.

Still, this case was more than just trying to get a predator off the streets to EP. This was the first time the Kidder name had been thrust into a negative spotlight, and it was his fault, naturally. His father's glare slapped him in the face and left a sting reminiscent of a surprising December cold wave captivating the state of Florida when the family got together for their traditional Sunday evening cookouts. His father's look always spoke a thousand words.

But he knew his stint with the Sheriff's Department was only temporary. He needed to build a resume of public service, albeit a positive and unblemished one that would eventually carry him into the glamorous world of local politics. His father, Stephen Kidder, a former deputy, now dominated city hall as the City Manager. His grandfather and great-grandfather, also former police officials, held the rank of Mayor and Sheriff. And EP was expected, fittingly, to follow in their footsteps. One day, it would be up to him to bring more glory and public service to the community, to keep the Kidder name in the spotlight, that's what it was all about in the end, and then his children and their children would eventually follow suit. That was the plan anyway.

In St. Augustine, it was pretty simple. If your last name was Kidder, and you were on a ballot, you were guaranteed to win the election. The name was sacred, legendary, and until now without blemish, precisely why a news story of a serial killer, with a Kidder as lead detective, was not acceptable front page material.

And the killer, to date, was smarter than him.

The killer did not *care* about the Kidder family name, the legacy, or the dynasty he was destroying when he abducted young women and robbed them of their lives. And as EP poured himself another cup of coffee, patiently waiting for the special agent from the FBI to arrive, he knew that was one thing he had that the killer did not.

He *cared*.

He was also a Kidder, and took the good with

bad gracefully.

Ernest Paul Kidder had all the connections, all right, but on the brink nonetheless.

*

The first thing Special Agent Mahan Pierce noticed while driving towards the St. John's County Sheriff's Office was that St. Augustine was indeed an ancient city. The streetlights were far too dim, reminding her of neighborhoods built during the 80's and 90's. Every intersection appeared unsafe, and the lighting was a useless deterrent for crime of any level.

The roads were narrow, and light yellow stripes marked the way along cemented roadways. *Unsafe*, she thought while making a mental note to not vote for whoever was in charge of the city if God forbid she ever had to call St. Augustine home. She had to remind herself things were different here, in the South. She was from the upper East Coast, New York, where things were bigger, better, and in this case, more advanced, or so she thought.

The weather was different here too.

There was a slight chill in the air when she departed from JFK that evening, but she found herself removing her windbreaker before she even reached the stairs leading into the Sheriff's Office as the muggy Southern air consumed her like mist from Niagara Falls. She couldn't believe a layer of sweat had formed in such a short walk, but now her clothes stuck to her like a pair of wet socks.

And then an annoying twist of fate set her off.

Entering the building, the air conditioner startled her, and the layer of sweat brought on a bitter chill. It almost forced her to put the windbreaker back on.

"Jesus Christ," she said aloud after observing no one was near. "Can't these people figure anything out?" She did not mean anything by her words, knew it was her job to go and help authorities wherever, and whenever needed, she just hated the calls that came last minute, so it was easy to find things to bitch about. And it never failed. Those calls only came on holidays, when plans and other arrangements had already been made, as in this case, when she had to leave her brother and sister behind at her home with no time frame on when she might return.

It was her fault though, she knew.

No one twisted her arm when she chose this particular career path. With a Ph.D. in biology from Cornell University, and with junior degrees in Criminal Justice and Crime Scene Analysis, she never even thought about applying to the FBI. Instead, they had diligently recruited her, convincingly enough to where in the end; she had left the meeting thinking she really did not have any other choice. Getting into the mind of a killer was her calling.

She was good at it, that's what *everyone* said anyway.

Maybe there had been *some* arm twisting after all, she admitted.

And now she was in St. Augustine, where somewhere out there, hidden in the shadows, a killer was lurking, and preparing to strike again.

2

Detective Kidder noticed Special Agent Pierce the instant the elevator doors opened. Reminiscent of a *Leo* diamond, she flawlessly wore a pair of tight fitting denim blue jeans. A plain white long-sleeved top draped from her shoulders and a windbreaker was tucked underneath her left arm. *It's July, why would she need a windbreaker in Florida?* Her skin was olive, lips full and equal. Her eyes were hazel, but dark green colors were more dominant than anything else, and her hair was dark brown, straightened manually. She was stunning, even her walk encompassed a natural confidence she must have been born with and Kidder noticed his fellow colleagues staring at her as she made her way toward him. His first thought, *she can't be my liaison from the Bureau.* FBI credentials hung from the belt around her fit midsection, however, and left no doubt of her status within the national crime fighting organization.

"Agent Pierce," he began, stood from behind his desk and extended his hand, hiding his amazement, along with his arousal. "Glad you could come. Sorry to get you on a holiday and all...."

"Glad to be here," she responded plainly, fanning herself with her shirt. He had not succeeded in hiding anything; his demeanor had been clear since the elevator doors opened. Mahan was used to men and women finding her attractive. She actually kind of liked it, often using it to her advantage. She also found Kidder's handsomeness surprising, but was far better at hiding the thoughts outlining her wayward id. Smiling both inside and out, she never took a seat, nor let her chaperon continue. She needed a drink. "What do you say we get out of here and introduce ourselves over a drink and maybe an appetizer of some crab claws I keep hearing so much about?"

Kidder found the question odd, but agreed anyway and quickly removed himself from behind his desk. He never noticed the eyes of his constituents as they watched him walk briskly after the woman who was already halfway back to the elevators.

The doors opened just as he caught up.

"You don't waste anytime do you?" he asked, surprisingly a bit fatigued.

"No, it's not that," Mahan responded with a smirk as she stood in front of him with her back turned. EP could not see the grin outlining her face. "I just always get what I want."

"Is that so?"

"Yes Detective Kidder, it is."

"And what is it that you want?"

"I've already told you," Mahan answered just as the elevator doors closed. "A drink and some crab claws. I'm assuming you know a good spot?"

*

Freezing cold, the room at the Ramada Inn felt Antarctic.

Abraham liked it that way.

He shivered under the covers as he lay there in the dark. The window air conditioning unit had been set to the lowest temperature, and the outdated solid green curtains were drawn to a close over the single window, except for an inch by the edge. Abraham wanted to see outside, the shadows, the life. The cold air made his body tremble, no matter how snug he was beneath the covers, and every time he saw a girl's shadow infiltrate the room, the anticipation of what he was about to do mounted.

Unaware of the danger lurking inside, people passed his room all night

Finally, he could not take it anymore.

The itch was back in full throttle, and he wanted to climb from beneath the covers, stark naked, and simply open the door and grab the next person to walk by.

But he could not, would not.

It was not the Fourth of July.

So, even though he knew he would have to pay for it, he found a suitable pornographic movie on the television.

He needed to make one more stop at the checkout counter tomorrow anyway.

His plan was already in motion.

And he masturbated three more times before drifting into a peaceful slumber.

*

The restaurant was cozy, quiet and the view of the Atlantic coastline reiterated perfection.

Fiddler's Green was just over the bridge off San Marco, two miles away from the Sheriff's Department and located right on the coastline of Vilano Beach. It was also one of the only places Detective Kidder thought might be quiet enough for the two of them to talk. Surprisingly, the restaurant had remained a well-kept secret from the nosy tourists infiltrating the area this time of year, and many people simply could not afford to dine there. Still, even though the tables were trimmed in candlelight, the aura in the air was not that of romance, but of business, and apparently to satisfy the hunger of Special Agent Pierce.

"Two dirty martinis and an order of your fried crab claws," Mahan spoke before the waiter made his introduction. The waiter walked away, but Kidder's eyes still had a lot to offer. "What? You do drink martini's don't you Detective Kidder?"

"Can't say I ever have," he replied. "Beach bums like yours truly prefer a cold beer most of the time. But since we're splitting the check, I think I will. And please," he added, not sure if he was able to take charge of the conversation, but happy nonetheless to complete a sentence. "Call me EP."

"Okay EP," she fired back placing the napkin in her lap, while her counterpart left his silverware rolled and untouched on the table. The comment he made of them splitting the check caught her off guard, but she liked it. She liked men that tried to take control. Very seldom was one able to do so, but she truly appreciated it. "Tell me what's going on in this lovely town of yours?" Then, she added silently, *lovely my ass. It's too hot and sticky.*

"I'm assuming you've already read the file so I'll keep it brief." EP unknowingly smirked, Mahan noticed. She started to wonder where his attitude came from, almost asked. She was sure he was hiding something behind his set of bluish gray eyes. His dark, jet-black hair had a slight curl, and she sensed it had recently been trimmed. He had a patch of hair on his chin, but the rest of his face was clean. He was tall, 6'1, maybe 6'2" and lean. He worked out, she could tell, but not to stay in shape. She knew it was probably to reduce stress. He looked tired, the case weighed heavily on his mind and shoulders. "We got two bodies, three others still missing, but all five went missing on the Fourth of July, one a year, starting five years ago. All were last seen at different locations around the city, his dumpsite is unknown, although we suspect he favors the St. John's River. Victimology tells us little except the victims are all less than 5'6" tall and weigh less than 150 lbs. Their hair color, eye color, social networks, and race do not fit a pattern of any kind. I don't even think this sonofabitch knows who he's going to kill until minutes before it happens."

"Well that's something," Mahan interrupted to sip her martini. Every detail counted.

"There wasn't much left of the two bodies recovered, although both were pulled from the St. John's River with similar injuries. We don't think all the women were disposed of the same way though, and there are literally hundreds of salt-water marshes around the area, not to mention countless miles of beaches he could've driven on to dispose of the other victims."

"I didn't know you could drive on the beaches in Florida."

"You can't on all of them, but here it's a major attraction, even though the beaches are closed at night. We just don't have the resources to patrol every inch."

"So it is your assumption some of the bodies are lost in the Atlantic Ocean shriveled up to the equivalent of fish food?"

"Shark food to be exact," EP looked ashen as the crab claws were placed in front of them. "But I'm not assuming anything. I hope we find the other women alive, but my gut tells me otherwise. If they were, there would be no need for him to continue abducting these women."

"He hasn't struck again yet has he?"

"No, but its only July 3rd," EP felt strongly she should already know this. The notes he sent her office were pristine, very thorough. "The women have only gone missing on the 4th. No exceptions."

"So your gut is telling you that he's going to strike again tomorrow?" Mahan asked although already knowing the answer. Her gut was telling her the same thing, and she began to notice a passion inside the young detective she was not expecting. He was close to the case, it bothered him having to use the FBI as a resource but he was willing to do anything to catch the illusive killer.

He nodded. "St. Augustine hasn't been through something like this since that maniac David Lindsey preyed upon the prostitutes in the area many years ago. He was a real animal."

"But he was caught," she reminded him with a smile as they shared a drink, she was familiar with the case. She always liked to throw in a positive before acknowledging the negative. She used the crab claws as a reference. They were positively delicious, but she felt she gained one pound with each dunk into the melted butter. "I do think you are right to trust your gut though. That's the one thing all of us in law enforcement must rely on. And I also unfortunately think you're right in this case."

"About what?"

"The rest of them are dead."

*

The grand finale of fireworks coincided with my own and I wiped the semen on a dirty shirt from the hamper in the corner of my room. Soon after I returned the magazines to their hiding spot behind the chest of drawers and then, a bit fatigued, went back downstairs to say goodbye to my relatives. My cousins wanted to stay the night, but my mother lied, a slight slur found in her voice at this point, telling them that I had a big day the next morning, that I'd volunteered to help clean up what was left of the Old Fort's lawn.

I was shocked everyone believed her, but they did, and within the hour they were gone.

I did not even bother to say goodbye.

My mother poured another drink and then bolted the front and rear doors. She started turning off all the lights downstairs and then motioned it was time for bed.

She was probably too drunk to talk.

I was too angry to give a damn, but went back to my room anyway, to wait for her.

I was alone with her again on another Fourth of July.

I was alone with my loving, nurturing mother.

A part of me thought there was a chance she would be too drunk to come for me that night. I thought maybe God might answer my prayers. Perhaps in his busy schedule he had finally gotten around to me. But I also found myself removing my clothes anyway, only because I did not want her to do it.

Naked, I crawled under the covers and waited for her.

Naked and cold I started thinking about what I could do to stop her.

But just as a thought entered my mind, I heard a creak coming from the floorboards down the hall.

A tear rolled down my cheek, and a wave of chills spackled my spine just as the door opened

<u>3</u>

July 4th.
5:00 A.M.
    No alarm clock needed, Abraham sprang out of bed as if alerted by the sound of an ear jolting fire alarm. He used his forearm to lean against the wall as he began his typical morning piss, and seemed unfazed by the burning sensation his urine made as it exited his penis due to the violent masturbation sessions he forced his body to sustain the night before.
    He made a complimentary pot of coffee, using a washcloth to hide his fingerprints as he filled the pot with water and opened the small bag of what was supposedly fresh Columbian coffee ground.
    It did not taste like it.
    He showered, shaved everything but his head, brushed his teeth, then removed the bed sheets from the bed, and threw them along with the towel he used and all the trash from the room in a pile by the door.
    He then went outside with a disposable cup of coffee in hand to smoke a cigarette and survey the parking lot around him.
    There was no one in sight.
    Everyone staying at the Ramada Inn was on vacation, and he knew no one woke up at 5:00 A.M. on vacation, especially not in the partying district of old St. Augustine. He peered around the corner towards an entrance to the lobby and saw a laundry hamper with other sheets already waiting to be washed.
    Perfect.
    He still had work to do, the security cameras, but needed some help.

His eyes worked swiftly for something useful, this was part of the plan he could not account for, but he was good at improvising. He saw a supply closet on the other side of the hall; with an empty mop bucket and mop sitting outside and a pair of vending machines were directly adjacent to them. He had never done what he was about to do before, but was sure it would work.

Quickly, he put out his cigarette, put the remains with all the other discarded butts in the zip-lock bag, then picked up his pile of dirty linens and trash and exited his room after placing his room key in his pocket. He wore a red ball cap and prescription less glasses. It was the only disguise he needed. He was at the laundry hamper in less than ten seconds, where he threw the towel and sheets in with all the others. He thought about placing his sheets on bottom, but changed his mind. He thought the linens on top would be the first to be washed. He actually wanted to burn them, but that was not an option.

Then he threw his trash in the nearest receptacle right beside the vending machines, retained the washcloth he used minutes earlier and grabbed the mop out of the bucket. Placing the top of the mop against the wall at an angle, he gripped it at its center, and then quickly raised the heel of his boot and pushed down hard. The snap was quick and the mop fell in two. Without looking to see if anyone saw what he was doing, he used the rag to wedge one half of the mop into the soda machine, and the other into the opening of the snack machine.

Afterwards he tossed the rag into the laundry hamper, then walked into the lobby opening the door with his shirt, and approached the front desk with a smile on his face. All of this had taken less than a minute. *This better work*, Abraham told himself as a groggy, overweight Spanish woman greeted him with an annoying look. *She hates her job,* he thought, *probably has three or four children at home she struggles to feed...shameful.* "Good morning," he spoke cheerfully as he surveyed the lobby for other signs of life. There was none, it was still too early.

"What can I do for you this morning?"

"Well, first you may want to walk out into the corridor real fast." He motioned towards the direction from which he entered. He was starting to set her up, and found his adrenaline pumping like an angry lioness protecting her cubs.

"What seems to be the problem?" the clerk asked, already planning to remove her buttocks from her seat and walk from behind the counter, but intentionally left out the title *sir* for having to get up.

"Looks like some kids vandalized the vending machines out there." The time was now. He knew she was falling for it. "It looks like they snapped a mop in two and crammed the broken pieces into the openings of the vending machines. The edges are sharp and could cut someone. I'm sure you're aware of the all the lawsuits going on in this country. I'm just trying to help out."

"Well thank you sir. I'll be right back." She figured his help warranted a *sir* this go around.

The woman walked from behind the counter and Abraham was behind it before she even reached the door. He kept his head low, and avoided looking towards the camera behind the front desk. The digital camera operating drive was in plain sight right behind the counter on a shelf adjacent to the desk. He ignored what was being recorded on the cameras and his eyes quickly scanned the receiver. He found the PLAY button, then the STOP button, and then he saw it. He pulled a napkin from his pocket and quickly pressed the RECORD button and to his delight, saw the red circle symbol disappear from the monitor screen.

The Ramada Inn was no longer under recorded video surveillance, and Abraham was back on the other side of the counter, tapes from the previous two days in his pocket, with thirty seconds to spare before the clerk reappeared.

"Sorry about that sir," she groaned as she waddled back to her seat, but resumed the term *sir*. "I keep telling my boss to put a camera out there, or to at least move the vending machines. People are always trying to shake them or break them to try and get free stuff. You Americans really like your junk food huh," she tried to shift her tiresome mood with a joke. No one ever laughed at her, but Abraham thought it was funny and let out a sincere giggle. He checked the cameras again and knew the crew would be too lazy to even notice the cameras were not recording until it was too late. "Anyway," the woman continued. "What can I do for you this early in the morning?"

"A couple of things actually," Abraham continued with his plan already in motion. "I've already paid for tonight in cash, but I'll actually be checking out soon after the fireworks extravaganza instead. I also spilled some wine on my linens and need them replaced ASAP. I've already put my dirty ones in the hamper outside. I'm a reporter and will be taking a nap before the showdown tonight. The sooner the better, tell the crew I'll leave a ten on the dresser by the television if they can have my room cleaned before noon."

"I think we can handle that, anything else?"

"Yes," he paused, forcing his face to look flustered. "I rented a movie last night from my room, and want to go ahead and pay for that with cash if at all possible. I'm a little embarrassed by the title, and was actually hoping a man would be working down here this morning, but just want to make sure that it does not get billed to my credit card. I prefer to pay everything cash." He lied, only rented the movie to have an excuse to visit the counter that morning, that and the credit card was stolen.

"No problem sir," the clerk winked at him. "And don't be ashamed of watching pornography, you'd be shocked at how much money this place makes off those dirty movies."

"Another American thing then I guess," Abraham added with a joke of his own.

"Si', just like the junk food," the woman's laugh was sweet and genuine. He would love to kill her. "What room number are you in?'

"I'm Mr. Cundy, room 102."

"Ok, that'll be $17.89 with tax." He handed her a twenty-dollar bill and accepted his change graciously. "And I'll make sure they clean your room inside and out before noon okay. Is there anything else you need this morning sir?"

"No, I think that's it. I just want to make sure nothing gets charged to my credit card."

"Nope, not unless you decide to rent some more dirty movies before you leave tonight. As of right now Mr. Cundy, you are free and clear."

"Thank you," Abraham concluded as he turned to trot off with an extra pep in his step. He wanted another cup of coffee. *Free and clear,* he replayed the receptionist's last words. *Music to my ears.*

*

"Okay," EP spoke loudly as the task force assembled in the briefing room. "Listen up people, today is the Fourth, and we all know what that means." He paused as Agent Pierce entered and silently stayed towards the back of the room. He could feel her eyes on him, on his lips. "We are now on high alert. Patrol has increased their number by fifty percent for tonight's fireworks show. Roadblocks will be set op on all the main roads from Ponce De Leon, to San Marco, and a few in between. No one will exit the vicinity of the Old Fort without having a flashlight shined in his or her face. Additionally, we'll have undercover officers among the crowd at the Fort, more blending in along St. George Street throughout the day, and at least one in every bar and restaurant from the Flagler Campus, to the beginning of the shopping district, to the point on Vilano Beach. We have to catch this bastard people. He's not going to stop until we do. Are there any questions?"

The room began to empty and Mahan approached him with a warm smile. "You're good with a crowd, a good leader, people seem to listen and respond to you. I guess it must run in the family huh?" Kidder winced at the mention of his family's political arsenal.

"So you've been doing a background check on me?" EP was not surprised, but acted angry nonetheless. "Shouldn't you be investigating other people?"

"Wasn't investigating anybody, just wanted to know a little more about the man I was sharing crab claws with."

"Be careful or you're going to create an obsession for those things."

"Don't worry. The Bureau doesn't pay me

enough for that. Besides, you have nothing to be ashamed of by your family's political dominance in this city. You guys are like the Kennedy's, only on a smaller, less lucrative scale." She tried the insult as a joke, but could tell EP was not in the mood. She knew he probably had not slept at all last night. "Why don't we go get a coffee and have lunch on St. George Street? I want to walk this guy's hunting ground."

"Never heard St. George St. referred to as a hunting ground?"

"But that's exactly what he's doing Detective Kidder. He's hunting."

*

An hour later, Mahan was shocked at how many people wedged their way into the quarter mile long shopping district known as St. George Street. It reminded her of Times Square in New York City, only what appeared to be a little less people trying to fit into an even smaller area. There simply wasn't enough room to support the mass, and although she would never say it to his face, she knew right away EP's efforts to assemble an undercover force along this Merchant's Way would prove fruitless. Her elbows and shoulders were introduced to complete strangers as she rounded each corner.

"He's here isn't he?" EP asked as they left one store, only to fall into another tourist trap selling the exact same t-shirts three feet away. "He's somewhere along this street right now isn't he?"

"Yes," Mahan agreed, the hairs on the back of her neck were erect with a fear that only came to her when she sensed danger near by. From the minute they parked their car and began mingling with the oblivious tourists and merchants of the area, the sensation was strong. "I can feel him."

"You can feel him?"

"Yes, in my gut. It's never lied to me. He's definitely in the vicinity." A thought seized her and she unknowingly grabbed his wrist and came to an abrupt stop. Why hadn't she thought of this before? "When your investigation started five years ago, were ALL the merchants, owners, venders, and employees of all these shops investigated? I'm talking about janitors, maintenance workers, anyone and everyone who may have had a reason to be here?"

"No," EP knew where she was going with this, and also knew she wouldn't like his answers. "But we did trace the victims' last steps as best we could and interviewed those particular stores and their employees extensively. But no one traveling or visiting with these women were around them the whole time, and when their financial backgrounds came back, there was nothing to suggest any of them shopped at the same store. And without any evidence suggesting otherwise, our efforts had to shift elsewhere."

"Do we know if the victims preferred cash transactions?"

"No, and there is no way to know that, none of their personal affects have ever been recovered. No receipts, nothing, and no credit card paper trails. The particular stores in question were also lacking video surveillance at the time. I'm telling you, it was a dead end."

"But now five years have passed, what may not have seemed relevant then, may be now. Are there people at the station that could start making calls?" Mahan was thinking now, she sensed a definite danger in St. Augustine, had her doubts at first with three bodies not recovered, but her gut now forced her to believe the worst. Nausea gripped her, not from an illness of any kind, but because at times like this her brain worked overtime.

"What do you need," EP already had his cell phone open. This was the side to Mahan he had been waiting to see.

"I need a list of every employee from every store and restaurant on St. George Street that has been employed with the same or different establishment for the past five years and beyond. That will assuredly cut whatever list you had five years ago in half." The confidence in her voice impressed EP.

"That's going to take some time."

"We have all day, nine hours until the BOOM BOOMS if I'm not mistaken," she referred to fireworks as a toddler may. "Plus we can help. Get your people at the station to call the first half of St. George Street closest to Flagler campus, and we'll take the second half."

"You want us to go door to door and ask questions?"

"Yes, unless you have anything better to do," Mahan responded with a tingle of excitement in her voice as they walked into yet another shop. EP followed her to the counter and listened. "Hi," she greeted the cashier cheerfully then watched the young girl's smile fade into that of concern as she flashed her badge. "Is your manager available?"

*

"Still doing the usual this July 4th Abe?"

Abraham hated it when people called him *Abe*, but knew his employer meant no harm or insult by it. Miguel Hampton wore his slouched, wrinkled sixty-year-old frame well. He walked slow and tired, always adjusting the garments beneath his overalls. His hair was gray, as was his beard that hid his wrinkles well, except for those that lived beneath his eyes. He had grown up in a poor family, times always appeared hard, but he had survived, although never really accomplishing much on his own. He ran his own handy man business and janitorial service from the bed of his 1975 Ford F150. No advertisement needed, Miguel had survived all these years from word of mouth, fair prices, and quality craftsmanship. It was a good thing too that people liked him, cause being of poor African-American and Cuban decent, he ignored workers compensation law, had no insurance, and had never made a tax payment to the Internal Revenue Service. His income level never raised any eyebrows, and he always paid Abraham in cash, which of course was okay with Abe. He hated paper trails.

    Still, Abraham could not recall him mentioning any friends before, and knew he had no family to speak of. That made him nosy at times, but Abraham had long ago learned to keep his elder boss at bay. In fact, even though they had been working together for the past eight years, very little had ever been shared about their personal lives, and even less known.

    "Are you ignoring me again Abe? I swear sometimes I think your head would fall off if it weren't attached to your shoulders. Don't know how I've put up with you for so long?"

    "I'm sorry Mr. Hampton," Abraham lied but wasn't worried. He knew his boss kept him around for the company. Loneliness appeared to be the only thing the two of them had in common. "You put up with me because I'm a good worker, and you do realize your head isn't necessarily attached to your shoulders don't you?"

"Oh my heavens here we go again. It was a figure of speech."

"That may be, but just so you know your head makes up your cranium-sound, also known as your skull and it's made up of twenty-two cranial bones that have fused over time to form immoveable joints. All of that is surrounded by muscle and cartilage and connected to your vertebrae or backbone."

"No shit Abe, I was just trying to say you are one strange sonofabitch. I watch Jeopardy too ya know! I'm old and fat, not old and stupid."

"I'm just saying your head can't actually fall off, someone or something would have to cut it off. And it would take a lot of force" He knew from experience and laughed as he grabbed the tools he would need from the back of Miguel's truck and placed them into the trunk of his gold Buick LeSabre. A wave of excitement momentarily crippled him as the thought of his previous five victims came rushing back.

Corrigan Mularkey. 16. Petite, with wavy blonde hair.
Heather Geeker. 22. Brunette, silky smooth tan skin.
Peighton Mercer. 21. Red hair, Boston accent, mother of two.
Cassie Povia. 16. White blonde hair, olive skin, and heavy makeup.
Sally Bay Fields. 19. Black, green eyes, vanilla scented skin.

Every detail, every plea to stop, every tear that fell from their eyes before he drained the life from their bodies was as vivid as it was the day he killed them. He held a hammer he favored in the palm of his hands and turned so that Mr. Hampton would not witness the bulge in his pants. He only had a couple of stops to make for work, and then it was back to the Ramada, where he knew his room would be clean.

"But to answer your question Mr. Hampton, yes I'll be doing the usual family thing. A bunch of relatives should be arriving within the next few hours. Haven't seen them since this time last year," his lies were believable.

"I see, well should be an easy day. I got a call from the manager of The Tavern, the local bar on St. George St. Two clogged toilets and apparently a pool of vomit. Says the place smells like rotten eggs. I'll take that one. You go check on a leaky faucet at the Pizza Parlor there on the strip, and a couple fluorescent light bulbs are out at the Thomas Kincaid gallery at the North end of St. George Street. Then don't bother checking in with me, just go be with your family." Abraham was about to climb into his car and head to St. George St. when Miguel called him back and approached him with something in his hand. It was a fifty-dollar bill.

"What's this for?"

"Just take it Abe. Call it a bonus."

'Bonus for what?"

"Being loyal to me, don't know where I'd be without you boy. You're a good kid.'

"I'll be thirty next year," Abraham pocketed the money.

"You'll still be a kid to me. Now get the hell out here, before I try and see just how hard it would be to rip that head of yours off."

"Funny," Abraham winked as he climbed in his car and stirred the engine. "I was thinking the exact same thing."

*

"We've been at it this for two hours and have five names," EP was not complaining, but he was worried they were not moving fast enough. "I think we should split up. I'll take the left side of the street, you hit up the right."

"You sure you're ready to venture out on your own," Mahan gave him an honest smile, and realized she wanted him to take her. The chase turned her on, and his blunt manner deserved a spot in her bed. He truly did not care who she was, wanted to be in control, and she wanted him to be.

"Funny. I think I'll be okay."

"Well give me the list and I'll contact the bureau to go ahead and get backgrounds started on these people."

"Why? You don't trust the St. John's County Sheriff's Office?"

"Actually no I don't," Mahan walked to meet him face to face. She felt his breath on her lips, and recognized the scent of Old Spice aftershave. He was barely in his thirties, yet chose the scent found in most retired men's medicine cabinets. "I don't trust them to thoroughly investigate these people. Everyone in that department is walking on eggshells because of this case. Let's face it. The case needs fresh eyes, without the political backdrop. It needs the FBI. Now," she paused to choose her words carefully. She wondered if he would flinch, or back away. "Do you have a problem with that Detective Kidder?"

He handed her the list of names and walked away.

He conceded this battle to Agent Pierce.
He did not have a problem with the FBI's

involvement.
He did not have a problem with Mahan's forwardness.
Nor did he feel intimidated by her intelligence.
He did, however, have a problem with her looks, the way her ass seemed to float in midair.
And the fact that he wanted to be inside of her he knew would eventually cause a problem.

*

EP and Agent Pierce were both exhausted and covered in sweat when they met at the north end of St. George St. three hours later. Famished and parched, both agreed to go home, shower and eat before returning to the station to get ready for St. Augustine's famous Fourth of July festivities.
"I hope this wasn't a waste of time," EP spoke turning the air conditioner to full blast.
"It's the little things that make the difference Kidder," Mahan loved his last name. She started saying her name with his last inside her head. *Mahan Kidder...Mahan Kidder.* There was a ring to it, she hated to admit. She was already hot, wanted him to kiss her.
"Ah fuck," EP yelled as he banged on the steering wheel. Pulling out of the parking lot they passed a van with the name MR. HAMPTON'S HANDYMAN & JANITORIAL SERVICE on its side.
Mahan's mood dissipated. "What's the problem?"
"Did you see that van?" Detective Kidder answered quickly, checking his rearview mirror and then jerked the steering wheel again. "We didn't even think to check out all of the local contractors and other vendors who do business down here on a daily

basis. We've overlooked a lot."

Mahan knew he was right, but was in the mood again.

"So we'll have some people make some more calls. This investigation is going to take some time. Did you get the number off the side of the van?"

"Yeah," EP said and wrote it down on an old receipt and shoved it into his pocket.

"Good, everything is going to work out. We have a lot of good people on our side. Try not to let it get to you. You have to stay focused."

"I am focused," EP replied slamming on the brakes at a yellow light he thought about chancing. "The problem is this mother fucker we're trying to catch is focused too." He didn't feel like talking anymore, and ignored the text message that just came from his father, the city manager, probably with more bullshit he did not have time to deal with right now.

*

Abraham was just finishing at the Pizza Parlor, handed the work order to the clerk and was about to walk out the front door, when the cheerful blonde from behind the counter called him back.

"Is something wrong?" he asked calmly, studying her looks like a judge at a beauty pageant.

"No, no, I'm just new here, it's my first day and I'm not sure what I'm supposed to do with this invoice?" Her smile was genuine, sincere, and her nervousness was raw with excitement. She didn't want to make a mistake her first day on the job. Abraham thought it was cute. She couldn't be more than twenty years old, not from St. Augustine, and probably a student at Flagler. She was perfect.

Then a customer brushed by him. No one ever

paid him any attention.

"Just give it to your manager," he spoke with a smile, hiding the fact that he wanted to kill her. "We'll be sending out another invoice closer to the end of the month." He turned to leave before he lost control. "Have a great 4th tonight." His dick was already throbbing.

"You too," the girl spoke cheerfully even though he was walking away. "And if you plan on drinking tonight, be careful. A cop was just in here asking all kinds of weird questions and there are going to be roadblocks all around San Marco to Ponce de Leon and beyond. Just a heads up."

"Thanks," Abraham breathed as he exited the store and smiled. "Thanks a lot."

That was information he needed.

He would have to work faster now.

He needed to get back to the Ramada.

Now he would have to take someone from there, and unfortunately, that meant he would have to miss the fireworks............

*

Haley Tidwell was pissed, extremely pissed off.

"Why the hell would you cheat on me with my best friend? You didn't think she would eventually tell me?"

Jesse did not know what to say, but no, her best friend felt just as bad as he did after it happened, and he actually did not think she would ever say anything. And now stuck in St. Augustine on a family vacation with Haley and her parents, all he could do was face the music, and he knew it was fixing to turn hardcore.

"And you did it on my 23rd birthday! What the

fuck Jesse?"

They were in an adjoining room from her parents, but if they were in the other room, Jesse was sure they could hear everything, and it was useless to try and get his girlfriend to calm down. Her best friend had actually come on to him, but he did not say no, and of course that was going to be useless information anyway. He didn't know what to say, but saying nothing at all was going to be just as bad as whatever he did say.

"Now you can't talk to me!" Haley was off the bed now, and launched her phone across the room. Her phone had been the source of all her newfound pain. She should have ignored her friend's phone call.

"It was 6 months ago Haley, a mistake, it meant nothing. I'm sorry."

"You're sorry," Haley stormed, grabbed her purse and phone, and then opened the door to their hotel room at the Ramada and prepared to make her exit. "You will be sorry. Fuck you!"

Jesse thought about going after her, but did not.

He should not have said anything at all and just accepted whatever abuse came his way, whatever abuse he deserved.

But the door was closed now.

He did not know where she was going, or what she was going to do.

Or that he would never see her again.

4

The humidity was thick, even with a coastal breeze, as people began pouring from their rooms at the Ramada to make the short walk to the Old Fort to watch the extraordinary fireworks display. Abraham leaned against the door to his room smoking a cigarette, watching and listening to the family oriented chatter of those that passed by.

People nodded to him as they strolled along, but most said nothing.

He liked it that way.

It took an hour for the sun to finally set, and Abraham remained outside his room, chain smoking as he watched and waited for the fireworks to begin and for anyone to emerge in the now deserted parking lot.

He heard a crackle, then a boom in the distance and caught a glimpse of patriotic lights over the trees.

The show had begun.

He knew he only had an hour, and as his excitement grew, his frustration mounted.

Then he heard a voice coming down the corridor right next to his room.

It was soft, yet sounded angry as it echoed off the cemented walls of the hallway. He turned and waited to see who emerged. Truly, he was waiting to see if she was alone. Because no one else was there, and if they were, they were not paying any attention to him. No one ever did.

*

"I just don't know how you guys could do this to me," Haley spoke louder than she intended, but she was buzzed, had spent the last hour at the hotel bar drowning in the misgivings of her friend's trust, and was now suffering through the agony of trying to understand her anger and sadness.

She emerged from the corridor and saw a faint glow of lights above the treetops. She knew her family was at the Old Fort, her boyfriend had probably gone with them, and she did not know why, but she wished he would not have left her all alone.

Then she remembered she had walked out on him, and should have.

Then, instinctively she simply hung up on her best friend, whom she decided was just as guilty as he was.

"Fuck my life!" she said aloud, not realizing it.

"What could possibly be so bad on the 4th of July?" The voice came from her right, and as Haley turned around a gorgeous blonde, well-built, younger looking guy was leaning against the door to his hotel room smoking a cigarette.

"You know," she hesitated at first to talk, but his eyes seemed harmless enough. "Typical bullshit, go on vacation with my boyfriend of three years and find out that he cheated on me with me best friend six months ago. I guess that can put a damper on the old family vacation don't you agree?"

"Can, I suppose," Abraham left his leaning position and walked towards this particular damsel in distress. He could tell she was attracted to him, they always were. He had to choose his next words carefully. "It doesn't have to though. Why aren't you down at the firework show?"

"I'm in town with my family." Haley, mesmerized by his eyes didn't cower away as he approached her. He was beautiful, easy to talk to, and she welcomed it. "And I'm sure he went with them. Just don't want to see him right now. What about you? Why aren't you down there?"

"I'm a local, seen it all a thousand times," Abraham answered quickly and knew his plan was going to work. "My aunt and uncle are in town with their two kids staying here and while they're at the Fort watching the show I just thought I'd stay behind and enjoy their booze. It's free for crying out loud, had the old family cookout earlier this afternoon."

"Must be nice, wish I had another drink."

"Well go right on inside and make you one. This is our room right here." Abraham spoke gently as he pulled another smoke from his pack and pointed to the door directly behind him. "I'll be right out here smoking when you're done, and I tell you what, I know of a secret most tourists don't."

"Oh yeah, what's that?"

"You can see the entire fireworks show from the third floor of this hotel, so go on inside make you a drink and we'll catch the end of the show. No one should be upset here tonight. It's America's birthday!"

Haley almost refused, although it would not have worked anyway, but she did have to pee. Walking towards the door she asked. "What do you have to drink anyway?"

"Bourbon, or vodka, your choice. And could you please bring me out my other pack of smokes, they'll be right there on the dresser. I'll meet you on the third floor. Oh, and don't forget to close the door all the way behind you, you never know what kind of crazy people are out there."

"Okay," she responded as she opened the door and prepared to enter the room. "What's your name anyway?" The vodka and bourbon were where she could see them, and she noticed an un-open pack of smokes close by. She'd be in and out in a jiffy, so she thought. "Don't stand me up."

"It's Michael," Abraham lied again, he thought about sticking with Ted, but assumed Michael was a more attractive name. "And I promise I won't."

Everything seemed okay as Haley walked into the room at the Ramada. Full of joy and glee, she never saw Abraham's shadow move into position.

*

The stream of urine echoed throughout the cold outdated bathroom, and Haley shivered as the last drops exited her bottom orifice. She quickly wiped, pulled up her skimpy faded jean shorts and then checked herself in the mirror before deciding to exit the chilly, bland brown and white tiled bathroom. She didn't have any make-up with her, but did take a moment to rummage her long crisp fingers through her wavy dirty-blonde hair annoyed that there wasn't a brush of any kind perched around the sink. In fact, there was no feminine or male products of any kind found in the bathroom. *His aunt must be a light traveler;* she noted grabbing the door handle. "This will just have to do," she spoke aloud, yet again to herself as she exited the bathroom.

She moved towards the dresser, still alone in the room, and decided to mix a concoction of Sprite and Vodka. The clear liquor was a cheap variety, but it didn't matter, she diluted it more with Sprite anyway, still feeling a bit woozy from the power drinking she had left behind at the hotel bar. She tasted it, and was satisfied. Then moved quickly to grab the pack of cigarettes and exit the room. She did not want to keep Michael waiting any longer, and had been able to hear the thunderous crackling of the fireworks show taking place down the street. She at least wanted to get to the third floor to witness the grand finale; she felt that was the only part of any Fourth of July celebration worth seeing anyway. Confident, and excited, she paused only for a second more to stare at her full body in the glass mirrored door of the closet.

    She moved her hips back and forth. She made sure her breasts were supported and perky.

    She looked good.

    She knew *Michael* would not be able to resist her.

    Abraham already did not want to.

    Then, as she turned to finally leave the room, she took one step when something alerted her to be careful.

    She had just met this guy, was already trusting him, and had no way of knowing if the vodka or sprite was spiked with anything.

    No one knew where she was, where she had been, or where she had just agreed to go.

    Suddenly, just as the excitement had grown moments ago, it began to fade into her afterthoughts and a sense of worry stepped in to take its place. *But Michael is okay,* she told herself as she began searching the room for anything to validate what he had told her in the parking lot. *He's a local, simply hanging out with his relatives from out of town, right?* She wanted to believe him as her eyes surveyed every inch of the small room. Her stomach tightened and her gut withered in doubt as she realized there was absolutely nothing to see. If two people were indeed staying in the room, with two children nonetheless, there was no trash on the floor, the nightstands were bare, even the trash cans were completely empty. The bed was made; pillows fluffed, and looked as if no one had lain on it in hours, if at all that day. There was no tourist memorabilia, no cooler, or bags of food. And there was supposed to be a woman staying in the room. Where were all the shoes? The luggage, where was the luggage? Save for the offered alcohol, there was nothing else in the room.

A moment ago, everything was fine, but suddenly, everything seemed terribly wrong.

She turned back towards the closet and saw her face ashen in fear. Without thinking, she pulled the sliding door aside and opened the closet, praying to find what she was looking for.

Surely, there had to be clothes, or suitcases, anything to set her mind at ease.

And there was.

Albeit only one.

And as she bent down to open it; her heart sank into her chest as she realized the brown leather suitcase was completely empty.

She heard the door close behind her and felt the vibration of determined footsteps charging toward her.

Helpless, Haley could not muster the strength to turn around and even try to ward off the imminent attack.

She felt a powerful left arm grab her across her arms and pulled her close beneath her breasts. She felt a right hand go over her mouth and nose cutting off her air supply. She tried to breathe, but her efforts were fruitless. Everything happened fast, within twenty seconds her world ceased to exist. Unknowingly, she continued to breathe in the odorless chlorophyll that saturated the rag pressed against her nose and mouth.

Within seconds her vision blurred.

Then her body went limp.

And finally, everything turned black.

"Go to sleep princess," Abraham whispered gently into Haley's ear as he slowly laid her on the floor and removed the empty suitcase from the closet. "You are mine now!"

*

He had to cram, twist the arms and legs unnaturally, but Abraham was sure he didn't break anything. She was going to be sore when she woke up, he was sure of that, but he also knew that when she found consciousness, being crammed into the old, but well-crafted Saddleback & Co leather suitcase would seem like a bitter sweet symphony compared to what he had in store for her. The suitcase was one of the few items he kept after his mother went away, it was older than he was, but perfect for his usage once a year. He was sweating slightly as he lifted the suitcase on its rollers, but could still hear the popping of the fireworks outside the room. He still had time. He pulled out a plastic bag from his pocket and put everything left in the room inside, emptied the drink Haley had made in the bathroom sink, and threw the empty cup into the bag as well.

He had to move fast.

Opening the door, a thick mass of Florida's scathing humidity slapped him in the face, and Abraham chastised himself for not thinking to find a closer parking spot once the tourists began filtering out earlier in the day. *Fucking moron,* he didn't call himself names often, but felt this particular situation warranted a verbal attack. Nonetheless, the gold Buick LeSabre was in sight, about thirty yards away, and he was there in less than a minute after waving to a young intoxicated couple who ran past him in the parking lot trying to get to the fireworks extravaganza before its completion.

The trunk opened with a push of a button, and with his heart thumping with a nervousness he usually did not feel, he used the surge of adrenaline to lift the suitcase off the ground and planted it on its side. He had poked a few holes into the leather with a knife when he first used it five years ago. He did not want to go through all this trouble, risk being caught, only to see his prey suffocate before getting them home. He then pulled a Tylenol bottle out of his pocket, opened it, and quickly discarded the remaining chloroform in the parking lot, and threw the empty container in the bushes in front of his car. He knew he would not need anymore tonight, but if he did, he knew he could always make more at home. *You can learn how to do anything on the internet these days*, he mused as he climbed into the driver seat and sprang the engine to life.

The fireworks were still going, but he was not in the clear yet.

He still had the roadblocks to deal with.

Abraham suspected the main intersections would be crawling with cops as he turned left onto San Marco Ave. and headed away from the *Old Fort*, Castillo de San Marcos, where St. Augustine's fireworks show was reaching its super-charged conclusion. He had mapped out his escape route earlier that afternoon using the city map of the phonebook in the motel room. If he was right, his route should horseshoe him safely around the cops, using dimly lit, quiet neighborhood streets for camouflage.

He traveled a block north, and already saw a faint glow of red and blue flashing lights ahead at the intersection of San Marco and A1A North, the connecting road to Vilano Beach.

He turned right onto Sebastian Ave. and then left onto Magnolia.

The streets were dark, quiet and flooded with single family homes. He hit a few stop signs, looked down the adjoining streets towards San Marco, and breathed a sigh of relief. There were no cops, there were not any cars at all, save for the few empty vehicles parked in front of the enchanting cottage styled homes. He continued north through a few more intersections, crossed over A1A N undetected, and finally came to an end at Magnolia Ave. He expected this, turned left back towards San Marco, but before he could get too close, made another right on a neighboring street. He was careful to do the speed limit, not wanting to draw any attention his way, and finally wound up at Milton St. Again, he turned left back towards San Marco. The intersection was in view, and he could not see any patrol cars up ahead. This was the only part that worried him. Abraham had no choice but to turn onto the heavily traveled San Marco, if only for an instant, but knew that if he could get through this intersection, he was home free.

He wrestled his gut to stay calm as he made a right onto San Marco.

He saw flashing lights in his rear-view mirror, but none ahead of him.

His plan worked, he had horseshoed the *piggies*.

But he wasn't finished. He still did not want to stay on San Marco too long.

Another neighborhood presented itself and he

made another right onto Macaris St., then hung a left on Douglas Ave and followed it until it came to an end. He made another left onto Hildreth Dr., and then found himself once again at San Marco, which had turned into State Highway 5A.

The flashing lights were well behind him.

Now he was on his own.

His speed increased when the road turned into Interstate 1, or Dixie Highway, and without hitting a single red-light, Abraham disappeared into the night, leaving the crowd at the Old Fort, and the surge of police officers in the distance.

He lived two miles ahead off of Lewis Speedway.

He turned left and within seconds, ironically passed the St. Johns County Jail on the right.

A cop was pulling out.

Abraham Kinsinger offered a friendly wave. The cop waved back.

He then rounded a dangerous bend in the road and turned on his blinker. His driveway was a dirt road easily missed by passersby, and his property was hidden by an overgrown bundle of boxwood and privet hedges, and an assortment of young and mature oak and pine trees.

He slammed the car in park and climbed out. He removed the stolen tag from his car and replaced it with his own. Opening the trunk, he leaned in and reached for the suitcase. The excitement was overwhelming. He couldn't help himself, and felt a warm burst of semen saturate his boxer briefs.

"Happy Fourth of July cocksuckers," he snickered aloud, directing the statement towards the cops trying to catch him. "Better luck catching me next year!"

Abraham knew Haley would wake soon.
He knew she would scream............he didn't care.
He knew how to shut her up.
He stirred a mixture of Clorox, acetone, and a handful of ice-cubes in a glass container. He had to let it sit for a while, and then cool it in the refrigerator for an hour or so. But after a ten minute search on the Internet, and after spending only $7.32 at a local hardware store, he had learned how to make chloroform. He discovered many uses for the internet over the years, mostly involving calluses along the ridgeline of his palms and a slight chafing whenever he squeezed his penis hard enough to cause friction. This always irritated him, but the soreness never stopped him, and he was just as willing to use his left hand, never favoring the right, when a superlative pornographic image lit up the screen of his laptop. But as he slid the concoction that would eventually separate into two different chemicals inside the refrigerator, he was sure he wouldn't need his laptop for a while.
The he heard a commotion coming from the baby monitor behind him.
Abraham had purchased a set of audio and video baby monitors from Radio Shack five years ago, he used them often, or whenever he brought a new visitor home.
He turned to the video monitor.
Haley was sitting up in bed, looking around the windowless room, searching for answers.
She groggily tried to slide off the bed, but soon realized her ankles were shackled to the bed frame.
She tried to free herself, and Abraham began

heading towards the room stark naked.
"Hello," he heard her call as he left the monitors behind him. "Is anybody there?"

*

The fireworks ended and Detective Kidder and Special Agent Pierce stalked St. George Street with meaningful steps.

The party was well under way.

People were everywhere.

"Zone 1," EP whispered into the microphone attached to his shirt collar as he adjusted his ear piece. "Got anything?"

"Not a thing sir," an officer in charge of roadblock responded right away. "Got nothing but party animals and families coming through this intersection." He was in charge of stopping motorists at the intersection of San Marco and A1A North. "We had to detain a couple of college kids for being way too intoxicated, but nothing out of the ordinary so far sir. No one has gotten through without being questioned as ordered."

EP ignored a *thank you*, and continued. "Zone 2. Got anything?"

"Nothing to report sir."

There were 15 roadblocks in all, and he contacted all of them, each time growing more impatient as the response remained the same.

They had nothing.

And Kidder knew they had succeeded in wasting a lot of time. *Damn.*

He directed his attention towards Mahan. "If we don't get anything in the next couple of hours, then I highly doubt we will get anything at all."

"Not true," Mahan saw his confidence

slipping. "If someone goes missing, we'll be getting a phone call sooner or later. Someone will be reporting a missing daughter or girlfriend by tomorrow morning I suspect."

"You think there's a chance he didn't come out of hiding this year?"

"No," Mahan admitted. In cases like this, experience taught her to expect the worst. "Unless he's dead, or incarcerated for another reason, I don't think he would have been able to control himself."

"This prick always seems to be one step ahead of us. He hides all year and then gets his rocks off by abducting innocent young girls." He paused, picturing the two victims found floating in the St. John's River. Corrigan Mularkey and Sally Bay Fields had been viciously beaten and tortured to death then dumped in the St. John's River and left for the occasional bull or tiger sharks to feed upon. Like garbage, they had been disposed of, arms and feet dismembered, eyes missing from their sockets, all their teeth knocked out, and multiple bruises and stab wounds were found all over their wrecked cadavers. The coroner found multiple broken bones in both victims, especially in the rib area, and Corrigan Mularkey's tongue had been cut out. Her body had been found last year, and Sally Bay Fields was discovered two years prior. He often wondered why the other three known victims were never discovered. He wondered now if they ever would be. *Were they discarded the same way?* "I'm sorry. I'm just not used to human beings behaving this way. I know it happens, and I know I'll never know why, but I can feel this *sicko* inside my head. I can feel him laughing at me."

"Well I'm used to people acting this way. It never gets easy, and there is no correct answer as to why." Mahan stopped walking, surveyed the crowd quickly before making direct eye contact with the troubled man before her. She wanted to kiss him, felt he wanted to kiss her too, knew they probably would eventually, but spoke again placing one hand on his broad shoulders. "But I can assure you one thing. He's not in hiding. He probably works in the community, is well liked by all who know him, and its got to be killing him that he has to keep this secret inside him, that he can't be who he is out in the open. He's blending in well."

"You think he's carrying something with him, some secret from his past that makes him kill?"

"I don't know?"

"You think he's been to a doctor, therapist for treatment?"

"I don't know."

"Do you think we're going to catch him?"

"I don't know," Mahan hated to admit for the third time.

"Goddamn it!" EP wore his emotions on his sleeve as he once again began moving through the crowd. "What the fuck do we know?"

*

It took a moment for Haley's eyes to adjust to the faint light of the room.

She was groggy, her muscles felt mushy, and it had taken all her strength to sit upright in the strange bed. She knew she must have been knocked out for a while, wondered where she was, how she got there, and why? She remembered the hotel room, but this was not it. There were no windows, and all the walls were blank and pasty white. There was a closet door that was closed, another door to the bedroom also closed, and except for the bed and the nightstand with a small lamp occupying the flat surface, there was nothing else in the room. And it was quiet, too quiet.

She tried to climb off the bed, almost tripped and crashed towards the floor as she became aware of the metal cuffs around her right ankle. She followed the chain all the way to the bottom of the metal bed frame. She could move, but only a foot away from the bed. She could not lift the bed either; the frame was bolted in place.

She tried to make sense of what was happening.

She tried to remember.

"Hello." she called out calmly, not wanting to show any signs of fear, and trying not to panic. "Is anybody there?"

No voice answered her.

But seconds later, she heard someone outside the door.

Whoever was there was unlocking the door from outside the room.

She realized that there was no lock inside the room, once again noticed the absence of windows.

Fear tried to seize her.

"Was wondering when you were going to wake up," she heard the voice as the door opened and a figure entered the room. "You've been out for a long time. By far longer than all the others I've had to put under."

*All the others…*Haley was worried now. *How many more were there? Where were they? What did he do to them? Who was he? What did he want?*

She started to remember something...................fighting with her boyfriend..........leaving..............getting drunk at the hotel bar..............on her way back to her room when she met a guy, this guy...............and his name was Michael. She tried hard to put it all together and felt a headache manipulating its way inside her temples. She remembered feeling like something was wrong after entering the room. She remembered hearing footsteps running behind her, and then nothing.

She looked into his lifeless eyes, and then noticed his body.

Michael was naked.

"Michael," she spoke faintly as she saw him making his way towards her and witnessed the erection that had formed instantly. "Michael..." She said his name again, her tone instinctively invoking a plea for mercy.

"My name isn't Michael," Abraham announced as he grabbed the chain grasping her ankle, harshly lifted it into the air and the force sent Haley tumbling backwards on the bed. He effortlessly positioned himself between her legs and pulled her close. She felt him on her, felt helpless, and for the first time realized that her clothes must've been removed while she was out. "It's Abraham," he snickered as he pressed his nose against her hair and breathed in a scent of Herbal Essence shampoo. He'd always liked that. "And don't you dare fucking think about fighting me or you will regret it!" That statement wasn't a warning or threat, it was a promise.

In an instant Haley Tidwell changed.

She closed her eyes as he began to have his way with her. She felt his hands wrap around her neck, and she struggled to breathe, but knew he would be done soon and that he would let go.

She remembered something from her past.
Something she had never told anyone.
Something she thought she had been able to

forget about.

But it was still there, had always been there in the back of her mind, just waiting for the right moment to resurface.

What were the odds?

"Don't worry," Haley spoke bravely, but hardly audible through the grunting of her attacker and the trapped air in her windpipe. "I w...wo...won't fight you." He finished, and then looked down at her. Balls of sweat dripped from his chin and hit her in the forehead. She returned the glance, life also drained from her eyes. "You can do whatever you want to me!"

Abraham slapped her hard across the face and it stung. Her ears popped from the blow, and she bit her tongue.

Abraham left the room out of breath and baffled.

He would not return that night.

He did not want to.

And that *really* pissed him off.

5

When my mother entered the room that night, I once again tried to convince myself that it was okay, that this was normal, the way it was supposed to be.

Of course I knew better.

I watched re-runs of Law & Order all the time, had been for years, and saw how fucked up kids got when their parents touched them in the private parts. I saw movies too, watched kids turn against their will into monsters because of the actions of the people that were supposed to give a fuck about them. And I tried, I did really, I tried not to blame the bitch now standing in my doorway. I wanted to blame my father. If he wouldn't have left, turned his back on us, then none of this would have ever happened. Mother would still be happy, she would have never came after me, and perhaps I would have never found those dirty magazines in the garage.

I didn't like my penis, hated it with a passion and wanted to cut it off.

And I didn't like the fact that it got hard when my mother came for me.

I tried to actually chop it off with a pair of scissors a couple of times but could never bring myself to do it.

Then, there are vaginas.

The ones in the magazines gave me pleasure, but not this one.

Not hers!

Nonetheless, she straddled me and fit me inside her. She began moving back and forth.

I was used to this.

"I'm sorry Abe," she would always say. I never believed her. "I love you Abraham!" I never believed

that bullshit either.

"I love you too," I would always reply. Hey, I had to, she was my mother, don't judge me.

Of course the one thing I kept from her was that a thought had crept into my mind that night.

It was a thought I couldn't dismiss, and had every intention on carrying it out.

I never told her that I was going to kill her...

*

The call came at 4:00 a.m.

A girl was missing.

Detective Kidder picked up Special Agent Pierce at the Quality Inn off Ponce de Leon, then swung into a nearby Dunkin Donuts for two much needed cups of coffee, and within seconds reached the Ramada Inn Hotel located at 116 San Marco Avenue, just a few blocks away from the Old Fort, where the fireworks had been ignited just a few hours ago. "If this is it, it's right in the vicinity of where you suspected someone would go missing," Mahan acknowledged as they turned into the Ramada parking lot and immediately saw four other patrol cars, lights flashing, and a couple more unmarked sedans parked in the loading zone. There wasn't any sign of the media present, but they both knew that if anyone had been monitoring the radio waves, it would not take long for a news crew to appear.

"It's also right in the middle of the roadblocks I mapped out," EP's voice was groggy. He had not slept, couldn't. "If this is the call we've been expecting, our guy has to know this area well. He had to know how to get around them." They climbed out of the car and were immediately met by another investigator assigned to assist EP in the case. "Let me have it Tuesday." The fat detective shook hands with EP, nodded towards Mahan and paused to take in the voluptuous nature of her breasts, then exhaled a deep breath and flipped open his notepad. His hair was dark brown, but sprouts of gray had crept into the sides of his head. He had a thick brown mustache that made his dark brown eyes seem even darker. His diet was horrible, and didn't seem to mind that his waist size continued to grow at an alarming rate. Tuesday was a nickname, given to him by all his comrades on the police force because he was known for calling in sick on Monday's. His work week always began on Tuesday. He was never sick of course, merely hung-over, too hung-over to function, or even climb out of bed. Tuesday was a binge drinker, he knew it, everyone knew it, but nobody seemed to care.

Luckily, it was Thursday, his drunkenness a distant memory, at least for the moment.

"We got one missing, ah what's her name," he paused to scroll his finger down the notepad. He was also lazy. EP never liked him much. "Haley Tidwell, 23 years old, in town with her parents and boyfriend for the July 4th celebration from Tallahassee. Parents names are Franklin and Molly Tidwell," he paused to turn and point towards three people standing next to one of the patrol cars talking with another officer. "Boyfriend's name is Jesse Moss. Claims he got into an argument with Haley earlier in the afternoon, she stormed off and none of them have heard from her since. Her cell phone is off, absolutely no contact."

"Did he say what the fight is about?" EP interjected taking a sip of coffee, and quickly surveyed the boyfriend no more than twenty yards away. He looked worried, faced the ground, and stood a noticeable distance away from the parents.

"The usual," Tuesday proceeded. "He cheated

on her with her best friend about six months ago. Best friend confessed to it right before the argument."

"He offered that information right away?" Mahan asked, also looking at the boyfriend.

"Yep."

"Any chance she just took off, met another guy, and has decided to get a little revenge by cheating on him? Some girls are vindictive like that ya know." Mahan noticed EP shift his eyes towards her as she made that statement. She smiled and then, "Well, *we* are."

"Parents swear their daughter would never do anything like that."

"That's what they all say," EP conjectured and caught a stern look from Mahan. Tuesday noticed the flirting and grunted. "Well, *they* do."

"Get a room for Christ's sake," Tuesday declared closing his notepad.

"Anything else?" EP asked, although he already knew the answer once the notepad was closed.

Tuesday shook his head. "I called you as soon as I got here. Wanted to wait and see how you wanted to play this."

"Let's interview them separately," Kidder quickly took command and began moving towards the worried threesome in the parking lot. "I'll take a run at the boyfriend. You take the father and riddle him in the lobby," he motioned towards Tuesday. "And Agent Pierce you take the mother up to the room and have a look around." They all nodded, and EP quickly continued. "Also, let's get the hotel manager down here if he's not here already. I want to talk to every employee that has worked in the last three days, especially the front desk clerks. Someone had to see something." He then noticed the security cameras above the front entrance. He knew the hotel was probably littered with them and motioned once again towards Tuesday. He enjoyed putting his ass to work. "Call our audio/video people, get em down here and confiscate this security system."

"You got it," Tuesday breathed in the aroma of Detective Kidder's coffee. "You wouldn't by any chance have brought me one?"

"Sorry, didn't cross my mind," EP admitted truthfully, then handed his cup to him anyway. "You can just have this one. There's no whiskey in it though."

"Fucking asshole!" Tuesday accepted the coffee and the joke at his expense.

"Does this mean you are going to take mine from me?" Mahan asked and extended her coffee towards EP.

He took it. "Thanks," he knew she was not expecting him to actually take it. "We got a long day ahead of us people, let's get to it."

Stunned, Mahan stopped in her tracks now deprived of caffeine. "Fucking asshole."

*

"Some of these questions are going to be difficult for you to answer," EP had taken Jesse over towards his unmarked car and allowed him to lean on the hood. "But it's very important that you answer them truthfully. The smallest detail might make all the difference in the world in these cases. You understand that?" The boyfriend nodded. "Just because you may not think some information is important, doesn't mean that we won't. I gotta know everything. And I'm going to trust you not to lie to me. Don't want to lie to me. Okay?"

"I understand." Jesse was nervous, scared,

blamed himself. "I want to help."

"What was the fight about?"

Jesse hesitated momentarily, found eye contact troublesome, but kept his word. "Six months ago, she and I had a fight about something stupid, don't remember exactly what it was, but she left a college party we were both attending back in Tallahassee. I wound up getting drunk, got upset, and well, you know, wound up *hooking up* with another girl."

"Her best friend?"

"Yeah, Nikki Baker. She was drunk too. We wound up being beer pong partners and one thing led to another. I know I screwed up. I'm an asshole."

EP was familiar with the beer pong drinking game. He even played it a couple times with fellow officers. It was competitive, fun, an excuse to drink more than you should. "Well, if you're an asshole, then trust me, there are millions of other guys out there in the club."

"I guess so."

"Okay, so she just found out yesterday afternoon? What time was that?"

"Yeah, I think around 3:00. Nikki called her, guess wanted to get it off her chest that we, ya know, hooked up. For the life of me I don't know why she would do that."

"Maybe the guilt was killing her...."

"It was killing me too," Jesse admitted shrugging his shoulders. "But I guess I was just afraid of hurting her. I didn't want to lose her."

EP believed him, his body language showed regret and his eyes housed the worry of a concerned boyfriend. He continued to question Jesse further, but was sure that whatever happened to Haley Tidwell after their argument, Jesse Moss had nothing to do with it.

*

Molly Tidwell's cell phone rang in the hotel room and Mahan noticed the woman's hands tremble as she viewed the caller I.D. She was hoping it would be Haley calling to let them know that everything was okay, that she was alive and well. Then, a tear fell and she placed the phone at her side and looked helplessly at Mahan. It hadn't been her daughter, and the reality of the situation crippled her, a large lump formed in the back of her throat.

"Do you need to take that?" Mahan asked soothingly as she took a moment to survey the room which Haley and her boyfriend were sharing.

Molly shook her head. "No, no. It's my mother. I can call her when we're finished. I just can't believe this is happening."

"I can assure you we are going to do everything to try and get your daughter back." She paused as Molly wiped the tears away from her eyes. The room was clean, looked like all of Haley's clothes were accounted for. The bathroom door was open, and Mahan noticed a make-up bag, hair dryer, and curling iron sitting on the bathroom counter. It did not appear that Haley had left with anything but her purse and cell phone. "I'm sorry but I need to ask you about the last time you saw your daughter."

"Oh God!" Molly felt herself losing it. Felt everything slipping away. "It was yesterday morning, the four of us had breakfast down in the hotel cafe. Everything seemed okay. Then Frank and I went shopping on St. George St. and I thought Haley and Jesse were going to just hang around the pool that afternoon. We had all planned to meet up later that evening and go watch the fireworks together. We, I'm sorry my husband and I never saw her after breakfast, but when we got back to our room..." she paused and motioned towards the adjoining door along the wall of the hotel room. "Well, we heard her yelling at Jesse."

"Did you hear what was said?"

"I didn't really hear Jesse say anything at all, but Haley was obviously upset with him. Couldn't make out the words, but she was very angry."

"How long would you say the argument lasted?"

"Not long," Molly noticed Mahan walking around the room, observing everything. It made her uncomfortable, but knew it must be necessary. "Maybe a minute or two at the most, and then we heard the door slam. My daughter has a pretty hefty temper, explosive even, and I don't know where she got it from, but I've learned that when she's upset it's best to give her a few minutes before trying to console her. So, I waited and then I knocked on the adjoining door a few seconds after and Jesse answered. He told me what the fight was about, told me what he had done with her best friend Nikki, and well, he just stood there looking pale and upset."

Mahan didn't notice any blood in the room. There was no sign of a struggle. "Did he go after her?"

"No," Molly shook her head again. "He stayed with us, constantly apologizing for what he did, and helped us try and reach her the rest of the night. Frank said for us not to worry. That she probably just needed to blow off some steam and that she'd be back......but of course she never came back, and she hasn't answered her phone." Molly thought about her daughter and wondered if it was more of a case of *couldn't* answer the phone instead of *wouldn't*. "Oh my God," she buried her head into the palms of her hands momentarily and then continued to sob as she looked into Mahan's eyes. "Do you know what's happened to my baby?"

"No," Mahan hated to admit. She had an idea of her daughter's fate, but did not want to say.................

*

Tuesday did not like Franklin Tidwell's demeanor. Something was not sitting right with him. The towering figure was balding, but he was slender and had kept himself in shape over the years. He nervously scratched his arms with large hands, using enough force to turn his knuckles sandy white. His forehead glistened with a layer of sweat, and although he did his best to look Tuesday in the eye, they instinctively kept drifting beyond his head and off into the distance.

"You need anything?" Tuesday asked, but Mr. Tidwell declined.

"I want my daughter back."

"We're doing everything we can sir," Tuesday extended his hand, Franklin's grip was powerful. "I'm detective Jimmy Kantz," he went with his real name instead of his nickname, even though there were times where he was drunk enough to forget who he was all together. "I know this is a difficult time for you and your family, but I need to ask you some questions okay?"

"I'll help you any way I can."

"Good, can you tell me about the relationship you had with your daughter?"

"Hey!" Franklin stood up and glared into Tuesday's eyes with an intense gaze fueled by anger.

"What kind of question is that?"

"An important one," Tuesday remained calm, seated, purposely ruffling Mr. Tidwell's feathers. He was looking for a certain reaction. "Do you mind returning to your seat Mr. Tidwell?"

Franklin held his gaze for a minute longer, and then retreated back into the chair in the hotel lobby.

He started speaking, and Tuesday scribbled more notes into his notepad.

But Franklin Tidwell never made eye contact.

And Tuesday Kantz was sure he was hiding something.

He did not like Franklin Tidwell at all.

*

Abraham watched Haley sleep from the video monitor.

He did not understand.

The others had been afraid of him, right up until he killed them.

He remembered their screams, their tears, their pleas for mercy.

He had a feeling Haley was different.

And he would not stand for it.

Bitch, he snarled as he climbed to his feet and once again made his way towards the bedroom. He grabbed a rusty box cutter along the way. *I'll give you something to scream about.*

<u>6</u>

"Where are you? I got something."

EP yawned as he listened to Tuesday's voice one the other end of his cell phone. He had not slept in over 48 hours, and as much as he wanted to rest his eyes, he knew the first few hours of any investigation were the most crucial. "I'm at the Quality Inn off Ponce de Leon. Room 221."

"You with Agent Pierce?"

"Yes."

"Should've known you lucky bastard."

"Knock it off Kantz. How far out are you?"

"Two minutes." The conversation ended.

"Who was that?" Mahan asked emerging from the bathroom dressed in a towel. Her dark brown hair was wet, and clung to the center of her back between her shoulder blades. Her complexion was colorless, but resembled models from an Oil of Olay commercial. She noticed Kidder's eyes flinch at the sight of her attire, and how they appeared to glue themselves to the shapely thighs below the towel line. "Sorry about how I'm dressed," she offered faintly, but turned to hide her smile. She knew she could have him any time she wanted. "It gets too hot in that bathroom when showering, almost suffocating."

"Don't mind me," EP was beginning to crave her. It had been a while since he felt this away about anyone. Still, a girl was missing, that had to be his focus. "But Tuesday's going to be here any second. He says he's got something for us."

Mahan disappeared back into the bathroom, only to emerge seconds later fully clothed in a pair of tight fitting blue jeans and a FBI t-shirt. Her hair still wet, she went to work brushing through hidden knots as they waited for Tuesday to arrive.

He was there a minute later and EP opened the door to let him in.

Tuesday noticed stuffiness in the room. Saw Mahan's wet hair and a thin fog emerging from the bathroom. He looked at EP inquisitively, smiled out of one corner of his mouth and then took a seat at the small cocktail table across from him. He threw a couple of manila folders towards EP.

"Let's have it."

"Hotel manager's name is Kelly Johnson. Got a list of all their employees, and highlighted those that worked the last two days, especially yesterday morning and evening." Tuesday paused and pushed one of the folders towards his superior. "He also gave me a list of names for all the guests that arrived within the past week. There's only a handful of people that checked out prior to the girl going missing, and about twenty or so still checked in."

"Anybody start looking at the video surveillance?" Mahan started the coffee maker.

"Yep, and you're not going to believe this shit," Tuesday shrugged his shoulders and openly laid his hands palms up on the small table. "Fucking Ramada's security wasn't recording. If something happened, we're not going to be able to see it."

"You got to be kidding me!" Kidder slid his fingers through his greasy hair. He needed a shower, and a power nap. "When was the last time it was recording?"

"Not sure yet, got Thomas at the Ramada though. He'll call as soon as he finds something. I questioned all the receptionists working the last few days and all of them swear they never left the front desk unattended and that they wouldn't have stopped the recording without the manager's approval. Truth is, none of them speak English all that well, and to be honest, I don't think any of them would know how to operate the security system."

"So that leaves the manager....Mr. Johnson?"

"I wish it were that easy. He's been on vacation all week with his family." Tuesday removed himself from the table and helped himself to a cup of coffee. "Swears the system was recording when he left."

"I'm going to want to talk to the front desk people anyway. Especially whoever was working yesterday?" EP noticed that Tuesday already had their names highlighted inside one of the folders. He had also run background checks on all of the Ramada's employees. "Impressive detective Kantz. Thanks." He wanted to speak with Marissa Felix and Joanie Hernandez right away. "Anything else?" he asked as he opened the other folder and began scanning the names of the hotel's guests.

"Yeah, bartender at the hotel remembers Haley Tidwell. Said she was obviously upset, and was taking it out on a bottle of vodka. Supposedly she was drinking pretty heavy for a couple of hours after the argument with her boyfriend."

"Great, so she was drunk." Mahan knew that made her even more vulnerable.

"Think we should entertain the possibility that she's sleeping off one hell of a hangover somewhere?" Detective Kantz looked into the coffee brew. He wanted something a little stronger. "Stranger things have happened."

"No," Kidder stood up and handed the folder to Mahan. He couldn't believe what he saw.

"What am I looking at?"

"That's a list of all the guests at the Ramada,

complete with their license plate numbers, vehicle descriptions and credit card information." EP was already heading towards the door. They had to move on this as soon as possible. He felt butterflies in his stomach, found a new wave of energy, and slapped Kantz on the back. "Stay on top of the security system Tuesday. And keep an eye on the father. Something about Franklin Tidwell rubbed me the wrong way too." He then paused in the open doorway and directed his attention back towards Mahan. "Look at the tenth name down. I can't believe it!"

Mahan couldn't either.

A man was registered to a room on the bottom floor, room 102.

He was registered under the name Ted Cundy.

Mahan read Detective Kidder's mind and followed him out of the room. She was on her phone a second later.

The name *Ted Cundy* had an eerie resemblance to *Ted Bundy*.

*

When Haley woke, her cheek was stuck to the bed sheet. The pool of blood had dried beneath her, and she began checking herself for injuries.

Abraham had cut her.

Her cheek hurt, her left breast also was sore from a tear caused by the box cutter, and she noticed a gash inside her left thigh.

Abraham had spared her from another rape session. He just wanted to torture her, to make her suffer, feel pain. She knew he wanted her to cry, to beg for mercy. But she had been cold, numb to the abuse, and succeeded in not letting him break her. As the blood flowed, and the beating ensued, her eyes had remained dry, and her mouth remained shut. She remembered him screaming at her, calling her names, yanking at her hair and slamming her head into the headboard. The violent outburst had left her barely conscious, and Abraham feeling tired and dizzy. He had once again left the room dumbfounded at Haley's demeanor, but she knew that he would be back.

And she had no idea how long she had been out.

She glanced around the room and saw the video monitor on the dresser.

She could feel him watching her.

She did not care.

Closing her eyes, she revisited the nightmare that had haunted her most of her life.

*

When he killed Cassie Povia, he told her she was about to die, and she did not want to.

She had fought him.

Her nails had dug into his flesh causing an arousal that he would remember forever. That was the last erection he ever experienced with her. He had kept her alive longer than all the others.

And after he was finished, he pressed the cold steel barrel of his revolver, a Colt .45, to the back of her head, and forced her to march in the depths of the Twelve Mile Swamp Conservation Area. Abraham never liked to travel far when disposing of a body. And the seldom used entrance to the swampland was only two miles away from his house, right off Lewis Speedway. The large basin swamp had many saltwater marshes to wade through. Abraham knew the area well and used to play in the protected land when he was a child. Because of that, he never hesitated to stray off the beaten path, confident he could always find his way back.

Two of his other victims, Heather Geeker and Peighton Mercer, had experienced their final moments in the Twelve Mile Swamp as well. Neither of their bodies had ever been discovered. They were protected in mud, hidden from the world.

The night Cassie Povia died was not any different.

The night was clear, but she still struggled with her footing.

Abraham's feet moved through the muck with an uncanny steadfastness. While Cassie had to grab onto the occasional live oak or water elm to keep her balance, he was able to weave through the smooth cord grass and saltworts with relative ease.

And once the mud had reached his knees, Abraham knew they had traveled far enough into the swamp.

It was here that he would kill her with his bare hands.

The life drained from Cassie's eyes as pressure was put on her neck and she tried to focus on the serenity of a full moon.

Except for one final scream, one final futile gasp of air, the night was silent, and the silence continued long after she had slipped away.

He didn't think her body would ever be discovered, but had used a pair of handheld pruning shears to remove her fingers anyway. In the event that her body was found, and detectives tried to piece together what had happened to her, he did not want them to find his flesh hidden underneath her fingernails.

He then placed his hands on her breasts and began pressing her into the mass of thick mud.

She disappeared into the muck staring up at Abraham with lifeless eyes.

And as he turned and began marching through the swampland back to the trail, he remembered thinking of how much he was going to miss her. Her, and the high pitch of her scream.

She had been his youngest victim at 16 years old.

So what the fuck was wrong with this one?

Abraham's reverie was shattered by the sound of Haley's voice coming through the baby monitor. "Abraham." She called his name as if they had been lifelong friends. "If you're not going to kill me today can I please have something to eat and drink?"

He glared into the video monitor not knowing what to do.

I should, he thought. *I should go in there right now and kill her!*

He opened the door a few seconds later and offered her a glass of water and a turkey and cheddar LunchAble.

"Thank you!"

"Look," Abraham snapped as he tried to force himself to retreat from the room. He was tired, and had to go to work. He knew the news would soon be covering her abduction and could not get caught up in doing anything out of the ordinary. Mr. Hampton was expecting him within the hour. "I'm not here to take care of you."

"I know," Haley gulped down the water in three gulps. She was still thirsty. "You want to kill me."

"Correction," his tone changed and he leaned forward to look into her eyes. She still had so much life in them. As if he had no affect on her whatsoever. "I am going to kill you!"

"I know," Haley repeated, then calmly turned away from him and faced the wall.

"And you're not afraid of me? You're not afraid of dying?"

"No," the vision of her nightmare returned. "I've been dead for years."

*

The hotel manager Kelly Johnson and the two front desk associates, Marissa Felix and Joanie Hernandez, were waiting for Kidder when he arrived back at the hotel. Riley Thomas had found the spot on the security system when the hotel was last under recorded surveillance and was waiting for EP behind the front counter. They had recovered tapes from July 2nd and beyond. "Manager says they change tapes every morning after the graveyard shift and Mrs. Hernandez says she took over for Mrs. Felix around 5:00 a.m. on the fourth, states she took the tape from the previous day and night out and put it on top of the receiver. She swears up and down that she put in a new tape and made sure it was recording. You can set this particular system to record directly to a hard drive and have that footage saved for up to five days, but that's not how this was being operated." Riley was tired, his back hurt, and he needed a break as he motioned towards the security system. "Instead all the footage was being recorded directly to video tapes and then saved for further use. And unfortunately, the tapes for July 3rd and 4th are nowhere to be found."

"So we got absolutely no footage from the last two days?" Riley shook his head, and saw the disbelief in Kidder's eyes. "All right, where is Mrs. Hernandez? I guess I'll start with her."

"She's back in the office with her boss, Mr. Johnson."

"Hang in there Riley, I may need you to go through the footage we do have with these two possible witnesses. If they remember anything at all, I'm going to need them to identify certain people on the guest list."

"Okay," Riley tried to sound enthusiastic. "Are you looking at someone already?"

"Yeah," EP grinned at the electronic junkie before answering. "Ted Bundy."

Bewildered, Riley could have sworn the infamous serial killer was dead.

He reached for the BlackBerry snug in his pocket and did a quick Google search. Within seconds he found the answer.

Sure enough, on January 24th 1989, Theodore Robert Bundy had been executed by the state of Florida.

"Fucking asshole!"

*

Joanie Hernandez wanted to go home. She was sorry that a girl was missing, understood that she was a possible witness. But she had three children of her own at home that needed taking care of. She had phoned her next door neighbors and asked them to sit with her children until she could get home, and although they agreed, she sensed their reluctance over the phone. Her children were not the best behaved kids on the block. Truth be told, they were more like a pack of rabid wolves. If anything, she knew this would be the first and last time her neighbors would agree to watch her children. Their grandmother even refused to baby-sit.

"I'm Detective Kidder," EP entered the office and his presence in the room forced her boss, Mr. Johnson and Joanie herself to shift in their seats. "But call me Ernest. I'm going to try and let you go as soon as possible, but you guys may have actually been a witness to a crime whether you know it or not."

"Is it true a girl went missing?" Joanie asked sympathetically.

"Yes."

"And she was taken from....from here?"

"We can't be a 100% sure of anything at the moment," EP hated to admit. "Could just be a runaway for all we know. But we're treating it like a kidnapping, and truly need your help in the investigation."

"Anything you need detective," Mr. Johnson offered from behind his cluttered desk. He wanted to seem important. "Anything at all. You'll have open access to all of our records and of course to *my* employees."

EP could think of a million smart ass comments to return to the dictating demeanor of the hotel manager, but before he could let one slip off his tongue, a knock at the door interrupted him and he turned to see Mahan enter the room. "Please tell me you got something."

"Guy is smart, I'll give him that," Mahan's praise was not meant to compliment the suspect, but it sounded that way nonetheless. She waited for EP to meet her in the hallway before continuing. He left the door cracked and the two fell into a whisper. He was not aware that Joanie and Kelly could still hear everything they would say. If so, the two would have kept the profanity to a minimum. "We got jack shit. Got forensics scouring the room he was staying in, hopefully something will turn up, but at first glance it's as clean as a whistle. The license plate number was from a stolen tag. A local by the name of Chad Ortega reported it stolen off his Jeep Cherokee three months ago from the McDonalds right around the corner on Ponce de Leon. Also, the fucking credit card he used to reserve the room was stolen from a lady who lives in Miami. She only used it for emergencies, and had no idea it was stolen until a few weeks ago when she needed to get some dental work done. Hotel doesn't have any records of the card being processed so this Ted Cundy asshole must have paid for everything is cash."

"All right, let's get someone to check out this Chad Ortega anyway. He's at least worth a look."

Mahan agreed. "Need any help with these two?" She motioned towards the cracked door and followed Kidder back inside. Before he could answer, however, a terrified Joanie Hernandez cleared her throat and spoke nervously.

"I'm sorry. I wasn't trying to pry, honest. But I couldn't help but hear everything from the hallway."

"It's all right," Mahan tried to comfort the distraught woman with a warm smile. "Do you know anything?"

"You mentioned a man's name....Ted Cundy."

"Yes, do you know him?" Mahan felt a glimmer of hope, and knew EP sensed it as well. They needed a break.

"Yes, I spoke with him yesterday morning."

"Would you recognize him?" The question was important, EP was already scrolling through his phone to find Riley Thomas's number.

"Yes. I remember everything."

7

When I finally grew balls big enough to kill my mother, I thought I had everything in order.

And I did, I was just being a pussy.

I was a pussy for three more years before I actually did it.

Had to have sex with her three more times before I finally did something about it.

The plan was simple. All I had to do was wait until she was finished with me. She always wanted another drink afterwards. I guess it helped her forget about the fact that she had touched me down there. I was a good son though. I even offered to make this particular drink for her. It was going to be the last drink she would ever enjoy, and I wanted it to be special. I wanted it to knock her out. She told me it was strong, but I knew she'd drink it anyway, and she did. I tiptoed down the hallway and checked on her a couple of times, but I could tell she was still awake. So I retreated back to my room, and waited.

A voice told me not to do it.

But I had to.

I already had everything I needed.

I had her cigarettes and a lighter.

I used her own pillow to suffocate her after she passed out.

I thought she would struggle more than she did, but in the end, it turned out that my mother was weak. Her spirit had broken down after my father left us years ago, and to be honest, it seemed as though she wanted to die.

I lit one of her cigarettes and placed it on the bed next to her head.

The first one didn't work.
So I tried again, and again.
I stayed in the room and watched the fire start.
I watched her burn.
I'll never forget the smell of her charred flesh and singed hair, it was amazing, a moment to hold dear forever.
And before I ran to the neighbor's house to call for help, I removed the filthy magazines from behind my dresser and put them back in the lawn mower bag, from which I had found them years ago.
I hoped nothing would happen to them!
I prayed for the fire truck to get there in time.

*

A set of knees pinned Haley to the bed.
It was dark, she could not see who was doing this to her, but she recognized the cologne.
"It's okay," the voice whispered. "I love you.................."

Haley woke from the nightmare still shackled to the bed, and remembered she was living through a second bout with terror. She had not seen or heard from Abraham in hours, knew he must be at work, but did not feel the need to try and escape. She knew her efforts would prove fruitless. Abraham was not the type to make mistakes and she knew he had successfully done this before. She knew no one had ever escaped. And she knew that Abraham was still going to try and break her. He would never be able too of course. Her spirit was mended, but it was already broken. There were ultimately no more tears to shed, and no reason to expect salvation.

She did toy with the notion of prayer, and

dismissed it after a brief debate inside her head.
There was no God.
There couldn't be.
And if there was, He was an asshole, she thought.
As for the devil, there was no need for debate, she was sure such a monster existed.
Only, she didn't award that honor to Abraham. Instead, she tagged that title to her father, Franklin Tidwell.
She hated him, and everything he did to her in the past.
And the only thing wrong with being shackled to the bed, she thought, was that she would not get the chance to seek revenge.
That troubled her, more so than her looming death.

*

"That's him!" Joanie was certain, and she realized for the first time that he had been the one to turn off the cameras and steal the missing surveillance tapes. The vandalism in the hallway the morning of the 4th had been nothing more than a ploy to remove her from behind the counter. "That sneaky son of a bitch."
There wasn't much to the picture, though, only a blurred image of *Ted Cundy* casually strolling through the lobby three days ago. The cameras were out of focus, and although there were some noticeable characteristics that EP could use, he knew the figure on the screen could not be positively identified. He also assumed the dark rimmed glasses and the Australian Jacaru leather outback hat was part of his disguise. The thought of releasing the image to the

media crossed his mind though, and he would. It may be the only shot they had at identifying the suspect. It was weak, but it was something.

It was a start.

"We should still get Mrs. Hernandez connected with a sketch artist. Might be able to get a clearer picture? The one on camera is shit."

"You okay with that Mrs. Hernandez?" She nodded, but Ernest wasn't going to let her say no anyway. "I'll call the station."

"And I'll check in with the task force to see if they've made any progress calling the local contractors and employees that serve the St. George St. location. Surely, a list of names must be forming by now."

And a few minutes and two page fax later, it was confirmed.

There was indeed a list.

Albeit, a long one.

*

"Does she hate us that much?" Molly Tidwell asked, speculating on the possibility of Haley willingly trying to disappear.

"If she hate's anybody, it's Jesse," Franklin countered, the Crown Royal Canadian whiskey he gulped was smooth. He spoke loudly, wanted Jesse to hear him in the adjoining room. He didn't care. He had no other choice. "He cheated on her with her best friend. Of course she needs time away."

"She knows we're supposed to leave tomorrow Frank! She would've called by now!"

"I'm not going to worry about anything until there's something to worry about Molly. Here, come have a drink?" Franklin sensed his nonchalant attitude upset his wife. But what was he supposed to do, tell her everything? Could he explain how he had found *their* daughter too beautiful to ignore? Or how Haley reminded him of how Molly herself had looked when they first met, before the boredom of reality set in, before years went by and her body changed into something the devil himself would pass on? He cringed at the sight of his wife. *I'm sorry for what I did*, he thought as he slurped down another shot. *I wasn't trying to hurt anybody. No harm, no foul.*

Nevertheless, Molly accepted a drink just as there was a knock on their hotel door.

Franklin hesitated, but had to answer, and reluctantly found detective Jimmy Kantz, *Tuesday*, in the doorway with a smug grin on his face. "Is this is a bad time?"

"Do you have news detective?" Franklin's voice hinted annoyance, and Tuesday caught it. He wasn't the type to back down. "Or just more questions?"

"Well Mr. Tidwell, as a detective I've learned the more questions I ask, the more answers I get, and I know you and your wife must be worried sick, but there's been a development and right now I think the two of you can help."

"All right," Franklin mused and stepped aside to let Kantz enter.

"After running a background check on your daughter, we've found out that she's been seeing a psychiatrist for the past five years. Getting a judge to forgo patient-Dr. confidentiality is going to be a pain in the ass, even in a case like this......"

"What are you getting at?" Franklin didn't know how to respond, but was shaken. He knew his daughter had grown old enough to fight him off, saw she had changed, even went along with her therapy, but had always told her she had no reason to tear the family apart. He had changed. He promised her and himself that he would never do it again.

"Well, she's your daughter." Kantz eyeballed Franklin firmly trying to get a read. "I'm just hoping the two of you can tell me what was troubling your daughter to the point where she needed therapy. Save me from trying to pull a cotter pin out of the mind of a shrink. So do either of you have anything to say?" He was tired of wasting time. It was way past time for his drink, and the fact the two of them were drinking in front of him wasn't helping much....at all.

Franklin started to answer but Molly grabbed his elbow and pulled him back. "Yes," she answered. "I know."

*

On the ninth annoying vibration, and after leaving Mahan at the station, he finally answered his father's call. "I'm doing everything I can dad. I'm using every resource available."

"The fucking media?" When the City Manager, Stephen Kidder, asked a question, it was never presented politely, especially to another family member. He was always right, and always would be. That was the Kidder way, and even Stephen Kidder had to retreat to second in the pecking order when his father spoke. "At least this holiday weekend is over, but the shit storm is still here. And it has *our* name written all over it!"

"The sketch being released is possibly one that someone in this town may recognize dad. It may be the only shot we have. I'm doing this whether you like it or not."

"We'll talk about this Sunday night son. You

are coming over for dinner aren't you? Your mother and grandfather are expecting you."

"I don't know. I'm kind of busy right now sir!" His tone was that of angry sarcasm, and EP knew he was probably the only person in St. Augustine that could openly speak to his father that way. "I'm right in the middle of this so called *shit storm*."

"I can have you pulled from this investigation son. With one damn phone call! You don't want to make enemies with your own father, or this town. I got pull. You don't!" He meant that as an insult. In his eyes, his son had yet to prove anything.

"And neither does this killer. He doesn't give a shit about our reputation, and quite frankly, neither do I. Haley Tidwell is the victim here, not our family name. And she may still be alive. I'm trying to find her before its too late. Why don't you give that some thought and get over yourself."

"You certain we got a problem?" Stephen had calmed down, but still needed a drink and was still uncertain. He had been brought up to speed with the circumstances surrounding the investigation and wanted to believe she simply ran away. However his stomach began churning before his son answered.

"I'm sure dad. Surveillance tapes at the Ramada from the past two days have been stolen, and presumably by a man who used the alias *Ted Cundy!*"

"Mother of God! Don't tell me we have another serial killer." The thought of William Darrell Lindsey resurfaced, he was the man connected with the killings of seven known prostitutes in the St. Augustine area from the early 1980's into the mid 1990's.

"I think we do," EP answered adamantly. There was no proof, but he was sure. "But we'll catch him..........or I'll never be mayor!"

"See you Sunday son, and I'll want a full report."

"Like you won't have one already."

After that exchange there was no way to tell which dead silence hit the others eardrum first!

*

Mahan should have gone home, but didn't.

Her mind slipped into overdrive. She had a hunch.

EP's organizational skills helped her rifle through old investigative reports. Each previous victim had been cataloged individually, but similarities noted and linked to each case were clear. Every lead, every reference, every aspect of each case had been documented and stored away in a file cabinet right next to his desk. She knew this case must've been haunting Kidder's psyche for the past five years. She could imagine the sleepless nights, the irritability, the helpless feeling of not doing enough, and the inability to establish a successful relationship. She had traveled down the same road many times before, and had learned to handle the staggering sense of despair. But the loneliness, she never forgot.

According to EP's reports, three of the previous five victims had been staying at a local St. Augustine hotel when they went missing.

Cassie Povia, 14, had been at 42 San Marco Ave. at the Comfort Suites with her parents.

Sally Bay Fields, 19, had been in a room with her boyfriend at the Scottish Inn, also located on San Marco Ave.

And Corrigan Mularkey, 16, had been with her mother, one block over, at the Holiday Inn & Suites, located at 1302 Ponce De Leon Blvd.

It was not known where Peighton Mercer, 21, and Heather Geeker, 22, were staying. It appeared as though the two of them had driven down from Jacksonville, thirty miles north of St. Augustine, to partake in the 4th of July celebration. Both lived in Jacksonville, and were last seen in bars with friends in the downtown historic district of St. Augustine.

She wasn't concerned with them at the moment.

But she did want to look at the guest logs from the previous hotels of the other three victims.

Detective Kidder did not disappoint.

Secured in the files of each individual victim were the lists of every registered guest at each hotel. She scanned the list of names at the Comfort Suites first, and paper clipped a picture of the victim, Cassie Povia, to the top left hand corner of the paper. It took her a while, but she found what she was looking for. She repeated the process with the list of names from the Scottish Inn, and used the eyes of Sally Bay Fields to guide her. The same happened for the list of names connected to Corrigan Mularkey at the Holiday Inn & Suites. Time passed swiftly, five hours to be exact, and as Mahan realized it was two o'clock in the morning, she leaned back in EP's chair, stretched her arms behind her head and looked at the three names she had jotted down with concern, but lined with a sense of triumph.

In Haley Tidwell's disappearance, a man had used the name *Ted Cundy*. She inferred Ted Bundy. The killer was amusing himself, she thought, or toying with them. She did not find it funny, or like being toyed with.

But he had been doing it all along.

Her gut instinct had been right again.

In the case of Cassie Povia, a man had registered under the name *Alvin Fish*. EP had never been able to locate this person and stolen credit cards were used to reserve the room. There had not been an operating security system at the Comfort Suites at the time of the Cassie's disappearance and all efforts to find Mr. Fish had failed. Mahan was sure now that *Alvin Fish* was a fake name, meant to resemble Albert Fish, a known serial killer/cannibal and child rapist convicted of three brutal crimes in the Washington D.C. and New York areas. There were presumably many more victims.

The next name on her list, *Gerald Ridgeway*, was easier to infer. Gary Ridgeway, a high profile serial killer from King County, Washington, had confessed to killing at least 60 women after he was caught. The Scottish Inn, also apparently troubled with faulty security cameras at the time of Corrigan Mularkey's abduction offered no visual evidence, and cash was used to reserve the room. No identification was asked for at time of check-in and the employee had been terminated for negligence pertaining to company policy and procedures.

The last name on her list was the trickiest. She had never heard of *Dennis Nader*, or anyone with a similar name. But after a lengthy internet search, one name surfaced, Dennis Rader. And he was convicted of killing ten people, mostly women, in Wichita, Kansas. Again, EP attempts at finding *Dennis Nader* crumbled.

Now, the list was right in front of her.
Ted Cundy.....Ted Bundy.
Alvin Fish.....Albert Fish.
Gerald Ridgeway.....Gary Ridgeway.
Dennis Nader.....Dennis Rader.
It was clear. The man they were looking for

was using names of convicted serial killers. He had read about them, researched them, and probably even tried mimicking their methods of torture and death. *Is he trying to perfect their craft*, she wondered. *Or create his own?*

There was a difference. The other's had been caught.

He was still out there...and very much in control.

"I'm getting close to you," Mahan spoke aloud and dialed Kidder's number to share her discovery.

In that instant, delirium triumphed over truth. She really didn't know who she was getting close to, how close she was, or how much her body yearned for a slumber.

*

When the phone rang, EP wanted to throw it across the room.

Hours ago, a shower helped clear his mind. A can of Campbell's Chunky bacon and potato soup settled his stomach, and a long blissful sip of Jameson's Irish whiskey helped endorse sleep. Now, all of it, for a lack of better words, was *toast.* Sitting upright, he removed the white down comforter already planning on having to leave his abode. No one called at 2:30 in the morning unless urgency foreshadowed sleep deprivation.

It was Mahan.

"You still at the station?"

"Yes. Come get me." Thrilled he answered. Mahan also wondered what his bed looked like. "You owe me a coffee anyway." *And a backrub!*

"Give me twenty minutes."

He dressed in jeans, a plain blue t-shirt,

attached his badge and gun to his belt buckle and then grabbed his keys and wallet from the nightstand.

He left behind all the papers he had pulled out of his pockets before showering. There was a bunch of receipts, gum rappers, and other useless papers that would eventually find their way into his bathroom trash can. But tucked in the middle was the piece of paper he had shoved into his pocket after writing down the name of a local contractor's business when he and Mahan left St. George Street on the afternoon of the 4th.

His scribble had faded slightly, but in blue ink still read:

        MR. HAMPTON'S HANDYMAN &
        JANITORIAL SERVICE

<u>8</u>

A rusty charcoal grill sat silently in the corner of the deck.

It was too hot to grill in Florida anyway.

The aroma of his mother's meatloaf filled the air as soon as EP stepped out of his pewter colored Chevy Tahoe and began walking up the driveway. He also noticed the heavy stench of one of his grandfather's cigars stemming from the backyard. He ignored the front door, slipped through the back gate and found his father and grandfather, Jacob Kidder, on the back deck. Mahan was there too and she noticed a glimmer of surprise in his eyes as he joined them. All three of them had cocktails in their hand. *How did she get here?*

"You surprised to see me?" Mahan's question prompted the two elder gentlemen to turn and welcome him.

"Ah, my grandson has finally made it." Jacob winked at Mahan. He was seventy-five years old, looked it, but still had a way with the women, and constantly thought with the smaller of his two heads. "He's the future of St. Augustine agent Pierce, going to make this old city thrive again."

"This city is fine the way it is," EP's father countered, removed himself from his chair, and approached his son with an extended hand. Stephen Kidder then lowered his voice so that only the two of them could hear. "Hope you don't mind my asking Mahan to join us. I've wanted to meet her since she arrived. She seems bright. The two of you are working well together I take it."

EP nodded. "I'm glad she's here."

"Good, now let's see about getting you a

drink." They momentarily left Mahan and Jacob on the deck and entered the house from the French doors on the deck. In the kitchen, Martha Kidder was busy whipping potatoes and picking the ends off a bundle of fresh green beans. She noticed her son instantly, grabbed him with a stream of motherly affection and planted a wet kiss on the side of his cheek.

"How are you Ernest?" Martha was a great mother and wife. She'd been a housewife her entire life and lived every moment to make a perfect home and to care for the family. She never forgot a birthday, or a memory for that matter, and always found time to endorse her love. "I know you're stressed up to the gullet with this case. But that Mahan sure seems spunky. Hopefully this whole terrible ordeal will all be over soon."

"We can hope..."

"But if you ask me, I think she's sweet on you Ernest. I see it in her eyes every time your father or grandfather mentions your name. There's a twinkle in there. I saw it."

"I'm not asking you mother." His father had returned with a drink, bourbon and ginger ale, and the two of them joined the party on the deck. They stayed there for thirty minutes talking about the case, until it was time for dinner, and then at the table, the conversation switched mostly to Mahan. EP found stories of her upbringing rather enjoyable. Her Italian family, her life, and her views and beliefs seemed contrite and pleasant. Then while he and Mahan helped his mother in the kitchen after dinner, Jacob exited citing his age, and a lonely dog he needed to tend to, and Stephen had another cigar on the deck. They said goodbye to his mother and then joined his father outside. He walked them to EP's car. "Thanks for having us dad." Mahan thought it cute that EP referred to his father as *dad*. His father nodded.

"You and Mrs. Kidder have a lovely home sir. I hope to be invited again." Mahan shook hands with St. Augustine's city manager and then climbed into the passenger seat and buckled herself in.

"It was our pleasure. And please," he spoke only to Mahan. "Call me Stephen when we're here. We can leave all the buearocratic bullshit for our day jobs. Deal?"

"Deal." Once they were on their way she turned towards EP and smiled. "Well that was fun. So that's him huh?" she asked, his father in her mind.

"Yep. That's the asshole that I'll never be good enough for. And that other asshole, well he's the horniest old man this side of the Mississippi. Grandmother died of a heart attack five years ago. She used to joke that his sex drive was going to kill her one day. And sure enough…….."

"You have got to be kidding me!" Mahan refused to believe it. "Your grandfather fucked your grandmother to death?" The two laughed simultaneously. It was a good story, just wasn't true. "You know what you should do?" she asked revisiting the comment about EP not living up to his father's expectations. "Just prove his ass wrong."

EP agreed. "Where am I taking you?"

"Let's go to your place and have a couple more drinks. I don't feel like staying at that ratty hotel alone tonight."

"Sounds good. I want to check in with Tuesday first. Hundreds of calls have been coming in since we released the sketch on the local news. And all I've got is Irish whiskey and maybe a beer or two. I hope that's ok. But I got one hell of a comfortable couch and plenty of pillows."

"Good," Mahan flipped open her phone to

reach her team back in Quantico. "Because you'll be sleeping on it!"

*

It looked like him, but some of the features were wrong. The chin was different from his; his was more round than square. And his cheeks were not as swollen as the sketch on television. They were firm and strong. His hair was more wavy than flat, and his eyes were big, just not as deep-set in the sockets like the picture portrayed. But the nose, well, Abraham had to give the artist credit, it was right on.

This was the third time he'd seen the sketch on television that afternoon. Had anyone called the hotline and given the cops his name, he wondered. He didn't have any friends, wasn't worried about that. But what if his boss had been watching, he thought, or one of his neighbors? What about family members? Even though he had not attempted to contact anyone in his bloodlines for years, would they point the finger at him if they saw the sketch?

Godamnit! He did not want cops getting close to him. He felt uneasy, a little rattled and pressure clung to his shoulders like static electricity.

This never happened before, and if he was not caught, he would make sure it would never happen again.

All the others had been caught. Bundy, Fish, Ridgeway, Nader and everyone else he studied had all gotten sloppy and made mistakes. And there were so many more like him in jail, because they let their urge control them. The others had gone through similar childhoods, and had grown into monsters, just like him. But he was different because he could feed his urge sparingly. He was more in control, or so he thought.

He looked at Haley on the monitor.

Asleep.

It can't end this soon, he thought as he turned off the television and made his way towards the room where he held Haley captive. *I'm not done with her yet.*

As the door closed behind him, Haley opened her eyes.

And almost smiled.............

*

"I can't believe you're taking my bed."

"Why not? I told you I was going to. Now shoo. We gotta get some sleep. Do you remember how many background checks we have to do tomorrow? And did I mention that I want to take the sketch and still shot from the surveillance tapes back down to St. George St. and see if anyone recognizes our *Mr. Cundy*?"

"Don't come down on me." EP was defensive, and still wanted in the bedroom. "I didn't tell you to drink my entire bottle of whiskey."

"No, but you helped. It's okay though, we needed to unwind. Been a long couple of days. I think our minds needed a release."

"And now it's time to sleep?"

"Exactly, so shoo Ernest Paul Kidder." He exited the room and closed the door behind him. She heard him holler "goodnight" from the hallway and she returned with "fuck you!" She sighed and rolled over to turn off the light on the nightstand, thinking she should have let him share the bed. It was, after all, his.

Nonetheless, as she reached for the light switch,

a few crumbled pieces of paper caught her eye. She didn't know why, but she looked through them as her eyes grew heavy from the potent Irish whiskey.

She found the paper with Mr. Hampton's business name and number on it.

It had not been on the list of contractors faxed from Quantico a few hours ago

She made a mental note to call Mr. Hampton tomorrow.

And then, Mahan fell asleep.

9

"Our guy is highly intelligent, possibly self-educated though, as he does not like or want to draw attention to himself. He's a white male, probably in his upper twenties to mid-thirties and is good looking. Attractive women want to talk to him. He's confident when it comes to women, and confident about killing them. But I don't think he kills them right away. He keeps them for some time, tortures them, and sexually assaults them until he gets bored. He also appears to have a fascination with other serial killers. We don't yet know if he's a copycat or just studying their craft, but we do know that he's made it a point to research their history. He may feel connected to them in someway. Namely, men such as Ted Bundy, Alvin Fish, Gary Ridgeway, and Dennis Nader we know he's familiar with. He used aliases similar to these men with three of the previous five victims and with Haley Tidwell as well. All of these men were from broken homes, without a father figure, and all experienced some form of childhood abuse. They were all predisposed to violence at an early age, and learned to accept deviant sexual behavior as a norm. They didn't view women as human beings, but objects and we have to believe that the man we're after has the same background. So from now on, as we derive a list of possible suspects and run background checks, let's push hard on those that fit this profile. Any background with divorced parents, or deceased parents, and any evidence of abuse are important. Any person previously incarcerated for a violent act is worth exploring and anything involving arson is also a warning sign along with cruelty to animals. Let's stick to the age median and stay after it. He knows this area well and probably pays attention to the media so he knows we're coming after him. This guy is not going to be easy to catch. But it's the little things that are going to make the difference in this case. So, let's get to it. All of you have a copy of our sketch, and it's been put in every patrol car in the city. The Florida Highway Patrol and FDLE, Florida Department of Law Enforcement, have also been alerted. Let's hit the streets hard. Let's make every phone call and bring Haley Tidwell back alive."

The task force exited the briefing room and EP heard murmurs amongst his peers and the shuffling of feet as he approached Mahan. Everyone was tired. "Need an aspirin?"

"Never gave a profile hung-over before," Mahan admitted and blushed slightly. She would do it all over again in a heartbeat though. Planned on it. Maybe convince EP to cook for her next time?

"You did fine." EP really believed it. "About that aspirin?" He handed her one.

"Thank you."

It helped.

*

Jesse Moss had returned to Tallahassee. There was nothing more he could do in St Augustine, and he could not bear the cold glare from Haley's father every time they shared the same room.

Now Franklin Tidwell felt the same icy stare from his wife, Molly.

"She's your fucking daughter Frank! How could you do this? That's our baby. How could you do this to us? What kind of sick man are you?"

"I'm sorry Molly." There were no words to ease his wife's pain. No way could she possibly understand, but coming clean with his wife had felt right. At least it did the other night after they got drunk and Kantz had left them alone. He was not so sure now. "I wasn't trying to hurt her, or this family. I love you both. I do." He still did not want the cops to know though. Prison was not a good place for men like him.

"Go to hell!"

"Molly, we can get through this. It stopped a long time ago. And Haley and I worked it out."

"Worked it out? Please tell me how an innocent girl can work something like that out? Father's are supposed to nurture, and care for their kids. Not *fuck* them!" A sharp pain thrashed between her temples and dizziness crippled her. She needed to lie down. "Just get out of here Frank! Leave me alone."

"Please honey, the cops we'll be coming by to check on us any minute. I need you in the right frame of mind. We can get past this, you'll see."

"And I need you to leave me the alone you bastard." Molly's tone was mellow but cold. "I should tell them everything."

"Please don't Molly! It would ruin me. It would ruin us. Nobody has to know."

Molly thought about the embarrassment that would seize their family if the secret came out. From top to bottom, it would tear them apart. She would not tell anybody right now. She just wanted her daughter back. But she reserved the right to change her mind, and told her husband so.

*

"Whatcha got Tuesday?"

"Just got done talking with a couple staying at the Ramada. They saw the sketch on the tube, and though both admit to being under the influence, they swear they saw a man matching the description walking through the parking lot at the time of the fireworks, rolling a large suitcase behind him. They didn't think anything of it at first, but then realized it seemed odd for someone to be hauling luggage to their car right in the middle of the fireworks show."

"Did they see his vehicle?"

"Nope."

"I'm going to want to talk to them." EP wrote down how he could reach them.

Kantz continued. "Explains why nobody saw her leave the hotel though."

"Makes sense." EP agreed and hung up. He looked over at Mahan, distraught.

"What is it?"

"Mother Fucker stuffed the poor girl into damn suitcase!"

*

EP and Mahan once again spent the next few hours walking down St George Street, asking store managers and employees to look at the composite sketch and the photo from the Ramada's security system. Mahan wanted EP's department to Photoshop the picture better. He assured her it was their best work, but it was not good enough for her so she emailed a copy to her office in Quantico to see what they could do with the image. However, she planned to have the case wrapped up before they could be of any help.

A few people faintly recognized the image, but could not be sure.

None had a name to go with the face.

And most did not know one way or the other.

She dialed EP's cell. They had split up. He answered on the second ring. "What's up?" He sounded tired. "Any luck?"

"No," Mahan needed food. "Let's grab a bite. What's good on this strip?"

"The Tavern."

She saw the sign in the distance. "Meet you there in 30 seconds."

*

They sat at the bar, ordered the house specialty, chili cheese fries and a couple of ice cold beers. Both agreed that bar food was tough to beat. They sat in silence for a while, each watching a different television set. EP paid attention to ESPN, while for some reason or another, Mahan dedicated her time to the weather channel. She wasn't interested or paying attention. Hunger had induced a hypnotic trance.

"I've always been a Miami Dolphin fan," EP broke the silence and shifted towards Mahan. "But they just haven't been able to get it together since Dan Marino retired. He never won a Super Bowl or anything, but at least they were making the playoffs."

"I'm sorry." Mahan knew she was about to get in trouble. "Who's Dan Marino?"

"Seriously?" Luckily the two of them were interrupted by the bartender with an enormous helping of chili, cheese, fries, sour cream, jalapenos, and any other ingredient known to clog arteries. "Heaven!" Unknowingly, EP put a copy of the sketch on the bar counter and began devouring *heaven*. The bartender came back to check on them a few minutes later and saw the drawing of the man. He asked if it was the guy he had seen on television, the one the police sought to question, perhaps in connection with the missing girl from the 4th. EP nodded, identified himself and displayed his badge. "Do you recognize him?"

"Not sure," the bartender admitted. "Does look familiar though. Hey Dave!" He called to another bartender at the other end of the bar. "Come take a look at this." Reluctantly, the other bartender came over to see what the commotion was about. "Don't we know this dude? I can't put my finger on it." He handed Dave the picture.

"Take your time," EP felt a twinge of excitement. "This is important."

"Yeah, does look kind of familiar."

"Has he worked here? Does he hang out here often?" Mahan had a lot more questions but kept it short. "Maybe done some maintenance or remodeling.......?"

"That's it," their bartender had grown excited. "I don't know his name, but it kind of looks like that younger dude that comes in here every once in a while with that older man. Aw shit, what's his name?" He looked at Dave. "You know dude, the handyman guy that comes and helps us fix all the shit the college kids from Flagler destroy?"

"Yeah," Dave saw it now. "I don't know his helper's name, but I think the other guy's name is, aw fuck, last name starts with an H I think?"

"Hampton?" Mahan asked and pulled the piece of paper from her pocket she had taken from EP's nightstand. EP didn't remember writing it, and knew it would have probably been thrown away. She winked at him, perhaps apologizing for snooping about his room.

"That's it," Dave felt rejuvenated and gave his counter part a high-five. "His name is Miguel Hampton. He runs this handyman service we use. If this is his helper, both dudes come in here all the time."

EP and Mahan got up to leave and EP threw a twenty dollar bill on the counter. "Keep the change!" Mahan was already on the phone dialing the number to Miguel Hampton's Handyman Service.

"It's on the house," Dave handed the money back. "Just go catch that scumbag!"

"Thanks. We will"

Mahan got a voicemail and waited for the message prompt. "Mr. Hampton, this is special agent Pierce with the Federal Bureau of Investigation. I'm working with the St John's County Sheriff's Department on a case that you may be able to help us with. Please call me back as soon as you get this message." She left her number and their pace quickened as they headed for the car.

"Should we wait for him to call back?" EP asked the question, but already knew the answer.

"No way. Let's go pay this guy a surprise visit." There was electricity in the air. "Can you feel it?"

EP could. And he loved the sensation.

<u>10</u>

Abraham was supposed to be working, but the job was not going to take very long, and Mr. Hampton's clients were not expecting him for another half hour anyway. So, he had time to *kill*. All he had to do was take measurements for a master bathroom and walk-in closet. The homeowner's wanted to upgrade to tile. Then he would write an estimate, and if they agreed on the price, he'd go to Lowe's and buy the materials needed for the job. The price would be agreed upon, always was. Mr. Hampton's prices were always far cheaper than the competition, and the two of them would have the job complete in no more than two days. These clients would refer them to their friends, and would call again themselves. It wasn't much, but it was a way to make a living. And of course the getting paid in cash arrangement was unbeatable.

Right now, however, his timing was impeccable.

Franklin Tidwell was standing outside his room on the second floor of the Ramada talking on his cell phone. There was no sign of Haley's mother. But Abraham did not care. He just wanted to watch Franklin for a moment, his movements, and his demeanor.

From his car across the street, he wondered, was he like his mother?

He felt his knuckles turn white as he clinched the steering wheel harshly and revered to his past. Anger began to boil inside him like a wildfire out of control. He had to control it. This was out of his norm.

Then, an unmarked police cruiser pulled into the parking lot and he watched a fat, balding cop dressed in a suit emerge and wave towards Franklin before mounting the stairs. Must be a detective, he thought, coming to inform the Tidwell's on the progress of the investigation.

He wondered how much they knew. Were they closing in on him?

He was smart enough to know it was time to leave.

And Abraham Kinsinger drove away before anyone noticed he was there.

*

"I was just about to call you back." Miguel was nervous when he saw Mahan and EP pull up in front of his shop. His Negro-Hispanic lineage was rifled with age, and his eyes twitched and hands trembled when he was nervous. He was nervous now, and did not bother hiding it.

"Sure you were." EP was harsh and moved close to the elderly man in front of him. "When the FBI or any police official tries to contact you, you call them back. Do you understand?" Miguel nodded, and took two steps back.

"What's this all about? Do I need an attorney?"

"I don't know," EP laughed a sarcastic melody and pressed forward. "Do you? Got to tell you though, asking for one isn't going to look good on you. And that's a fact!"

Mahan had not seen this side of EP before and interjected. She didn't want to scare Mr. Hampton into silence. "Sir, all we need is for you to take a look at a photo and tell us if you recognize the man in it." Miguel eased a bit, nodded, and took the picture out of her hand. He stared at it a long time, rubbed his lips together, still unable to control his trembling hands.

"Can't say I've seen this fella before."

"Look at it again! Think!" EP had grown impatient. It showed. He didn't want to bully an old man, but felt strongly they were on to something. "I need you to be sure."

"I'm sorry," Miguel handed the picture back to Mahan. "I swear I'm telling the truth. I don't recognize him. Don't know anyone who wears glasses like that!"

"The glasses could be part of a disguise. Try taking a look at it again and imagine it without the glasses." Mahan handed the sketch back to Miguel, and there he stood again, looking at it closely. Seconds passed slowly, and again he handed the picture back and looked at them. "Mr. Hampton?"

He shrugged his shoulders. "I don't know if I want to go getting anybody in trouble, but." His voice trailed. The look in EP's eyes told him he must continue. He did not have a choice. "But I guess it kind of looks like my helper. But not really, some of the characteristics just don't fit him. But I'm telling you both, he's a good kid. Ain't no way he's involved in nothing."

"We need a name!" EP moved closer. "And address."

"This boy is a good kid. What you want with him anyway?"

"Name!"

"Abraham Kinsinger. I call him Abe. He's a smart, delightful human being though. Bout to turn thirty soon, if I'm not mistaken. Been helping me with odds and ends for years now. Only person I've kept around for that long. We kinda bonded. He's like a son to me. I'd really like to know what this is about."

"Can't talk about that," Mahan interjected before EP tried demanding an address. "But please Mr. Hampton is there anything else you can tell us about him?"

"He's quiet, keeps to himself a lot. Smart as the dickens though. I tell him all the time he should stop wasting time with me and do something with his life. He likes what he does though, and an artist with his hands, real good with woodwork. Comes from a sad childhood though, always felt sorry for him in a way, though he's asked me not to."

"Go on."

"Father left him when he was a boy and then his ma died in a horrible fire years later when he was still up and coming. Don't know if he ever got over it, won't talk about it much. But he's got a kindness to him I ain't seen in a while, and has a kindred spirit that's just a blessing to be around. Whatever it is you think he's tied up in, I'd bet my bottom dollar you're mistaken. When I pass, I plan on leaving my business with him. Got no kids of my own. That's just how well I think of him. You all are wasting your time."

"We'll be the judge of that sir," EP had calmed but still wanted to move fast. "We need an address and a telephone number *please*?"

"Well look who grew manners all of a sudden." Miguel walked slowly behind his desk and opened a drawer. "Ain't got no phone number for Abe, he don't have no phone. Got an address though. He should be home by now I imagine." He wrote it down and handed it to EP. "You sure you can't tell me what this is all about?"

"Watch the news," EP answered and turned to leave. "We'll be in touch. May be back with a court order and go through your records. Can you tell us if he was around the St George St. area on the afternoon of July 4th?" Miguel confirmed they both were. They were in the car seconds later and Mahan had already called the station. They wanted to know everything there was to know about Abraham Kinsinger, and they wanted to know now. "He fits your profile." EP suggested as he punched in the address on the GPS. And Abraham did. Broken family, mother had died in a fire, presumably accidental, almost thirty years old, tragic childhood, etc. "I don't give a fuck what that old bastard says, I think this guy has something to hide. I can feel it. I mean, seriously, what kind of person in today's world doesn't have a goddamn telephone?"

"The kind who doesn't want to be bothered or found."

"Let's hit this guy hard. I don't want him pissing without feeling our presence."

"We still got a ways to go," Mahan breathed deep and took the safety off her firearm. "But this could be it."

11

"Welcome to the slums of St. Augustine." Entering this part of town, known locally as *Crack Head Corner*, EP decided to give Mahan a brief history lesson. His father and grandfather had done a remarkable job cleaning up the imploding infestation of prostitutes, drug dealers and addicts alike, but this part of town still accounted for s surplus of the poor. These people lived in poverty, paycheck to paycheck, and had to familiarize themselves with the laws of the streets. And it was here they expected to find their person of interest, Abraham Kinsinger.

"So David Lindsey *hunted* here?" Mahan referred to St. Augustine's infamous serial killer with interest, and took in the scene around her. "But he was caught in the Carolina's right?"

"Yeah," EP answered as they pulled into a rundown apartment complex. "That's the power of teamwork."

The complex was shoddy, smelled of mildew, and a faded green paint job decorated the exterior. Portable air conditioning units hung from the windows, and they were all turned on full blast. It was July in Florida after all, and the window units caused a low humming sound to cross the parking lot. The roof was original, and patches of shingles were missing. EP wondered what the tenants thought, wondered if they even noticed the drywall turning brown from moisture?

"This is the address?" Mahan asked and EP wondered why. "Because this guy is marginally, if not overly attractive. He's Caucasian, and young, and just doesn't seem like he'd fit in here. It would be hard for him to be a part of this community. I don't have a good feeling about this."

"Only one way to find out."

They climbed a cement laden set of stairs, passed three shoeless children in the hallway, none over the age of six, and knocked on door number 212. They heard shuffling from inside, waited a few seconds, and then silence consumed the room beyond the door. Someone did not want to answer. EP knocked again. "St. John's County Sheriff's Department!" He declared then ordered. "Open the door. We know you're in there." Both of them emptied their holsters.

"Hang on," the voice in the background sounded flustered, panicked, and then they heard a toilet flush.

"Let's move. We have probable cause. Could be flushing evidence?" Mahan stepped aside as EP prepared to kick in the door, but before he could lunge forward the door opened a crack, and a bewildered set of yellowish eyes stared at them. Their nostrils captured a hint of marijuana. There were definitely drugs in the room. The owner of the yellow eyes, a skinny teenaged black kid, asked them to produce their identifications and they did. "You need to let us inside or we'll come in forcefully."

"You got a warrant?" The question was put to them matter-of-factly. The kid was being a smart ass.

EP countered. "Don't need one. We smell narcotics. Step aside."

Reluctantly, the boy allowed them to enter. He was wearing nothing but a dirty pair of flannel boxers and a stained wife beater t-shirt. No shoes, no socks. "Awe man. Shit." The kid sat on the bed. "Yawl bustas really gonna trump my ass fo a little fucking weed? Ain't you got better shit to do?"

"Actually yes we do, so just take it easy we'll disappear. Ok?" Mahan followed EP's lead and continued after holstering her handgun. "What's your name kid?"

"Jerome."

"Jerome what?"

"Jerome Washington."

"How old are you Jerome?"

"19. Man, what's this all about anyway? Yall can't just come barging in niggas homes man. Shit ain't right. I got rights." He repeated himself, though heard. "I got rights dawg!"

"And you're high as a kite Jerome!" EP was pissed. He didn't have time for shenanigans. "I got the right to haul your ass to jail. That what you want…Jerome?"

"Na."

"Then answer the lady's questions and we'll leave. You won't see us again. Okay? Or do you really want us nosing around to figure out how you, at 19, can afford to live on your own?" Jerome agreed and Mahan continued. "Do you know this man?" She handed the sketch to Jerome.

"Hell yeah I know that busta. He's the cat that lived here before I got dis crib. Neighborhood folk picked on him a lot, but he seemed a'ight I guess. Kept to himself. Didn't come out much. Couple of punks robbed him a few times and guess he just couldn't take it no mo and moved out. I got friends that live in this complex, that's how I seen him around. They told me when he left and I jumped at the opportunity for this fine piece of real estate." They ignored the smartass in him.

"Do you know where he went?"

"No, that's all I know. Swear on my life."

They left after EP reminded Jerome to stay off drugs. "What now?"

"Drop me off at the station and I'll see what they've been able to dig up on Kinsinger. I'll also try to get a lock on a current address." EP nodded and stepped on the gas. He couldn't wait to get away from this part of town. He was glad he wasn't on the VICE squad anymore. "What about you?" Mahan could tell he was thinking about something.

"I'm going to get up with Tuesday and pay Mr. Hampton another visit. I don't like being fucking stonewalled!"

"Take it easy," Mahan grabbed his arm and squeezed. It was the first time she had done this. They both noticed. "He can still help us."

"I'll be okay," EP promised.

"Want to get up later for more drinks?"

"Sure, but you're buying this time." EP looked over and smiled. "You drink like a damn fish."

"It's a date."

*

Kantz had a nine year old driver's license photo of Abraham Kinsinger with him when EP picked him up. The license had been renewed online, picture never changed. But they compared it to the sketch anyway. Neither man was sure. "Shit Kidder," Tuesday nudged his partner. "A lot can change in nine years. Sketch could be off a bit too. Damn things aren't always accurate."

"Jimmy, we got to find this guy."

"We will. Got a few more people to look into as well. Got a list of perverts as long as my dick. Most have been *inside* for sexual battery, molestation, and stalking. Lots of sick people out there. But we got hits on quite a few people with a history of child abuse and criminal records."

"Going to be a long night."

"Isn't it always?"

They arrived at Miguel's shop just as he was climbing in his truck to leave. There was no sign of Abraham. "We got to talk Mr. Hampton." EP left the engine running. This was not going to take long. "You gave me a bogus address. You should really update your records. I'm sure the IRS will oblige if you want?"

"Now wait a minute." Miguel was scared. He did not want any trouble. He never paid taxes. Could not afford to. And he did not need the IRS snooping around. "I gave you the address he gave to me when he started working here. It's all I got."

"We don't believe it." Tuesday chimed in. "Surely you can give us something else."

"I can tell you where I have him scheduled to work tomorrow. We got a tile job to do."

"Go for it," EP grabbed his notepad. "And do not tell him we're coming, or we'll be back with the FEDS and a subpoena to go through your files." Miguel did not like being threatened, was not used it, but agreed nonetheless. "One more thing." EP turned to leave but thought of something else. "What kind of car does he drive?"

"Gold Buick LeSabre."

"Thank you Mr. Hampton. Enjoy your evening."

Miguel did not climb into his truck until they were gone. He felt uneasy, and wished Abraham had a phone.

His *son* was in trouble.

And regardless of what he just told Detective

Kidder, he would help him anyway he could.

*

The paranoia bothered him, but what could he do?

Think idiot. He tried to calm down, but there was no use. He looked out the window and down the driveway towards the road. Only his car was in the driveway, and there was not a soul in sight. But he could feel eyes on him, watching his every move. *Right?* He looked out the window again just as a car passed from the road. *Cops?* No, he had been careful, very careful. But then why were his instincts suggesting otherwise? The paranoia refused to subside.

There was only one answer.

Something was wrong, had to be.

He thought about Haley, knew he should kill her now and not waste anymore time. If the *piggies* were on to him, he knew he had to get rid of the body and clean the room before they found him.

He watched Haley from the monitor, feeling overwhelmed.

And, he felt something else, but could not make sense of it.

He was sure he had never felt it before.

Focus fuckwad. He was losing it. He had to be smart or everything would slip away. He did not want to wind up like all the others. He did not want to spend the rest of his life confined to a cell. *Then what are you waiting for*, he thought as his eyes drifted back to Haley Tidwell. *She's just like all the others. Her fate has already been decided.*

His dick was hard and he started to rub it.

He had to have her one more time before the

end came.

And this time would be special.

She's going to know, he believed as he made his way towards the bedroom. He thought about bringing a knife into the room, but talked himself out of it. *You don't need it to do her. Just use your hands.* He stripped stark naked before he reached the door, and stood there, his penis throbbing, trying to figure out another way. *You don't owe her anything. Cops are closer than they've ever been. This has to be done.*

"Abraham?" Haley's voice startled him. "Are you there?"

How had she known he was outside the door? Was he talking out loud? "Yes," Abraham answered, half choking on the word and opened the door revealing him to her. She did not cower away, however, or try to hide beneath the covers. She tried to speak but Abraham moved swiftly and was on top of her in seconds. His heart raced to the pace of a cocaine overdose and as his hands clasped around her throat, the unfamiliar feeling returned. *What the hell is going on?*

She took small breaths. He allowed her too.

But time was running out.

He loved being inside her.

He loved looking into her eyes as he panted over her. Her taste, smell, the silkiness of her skin, and her perfect nipples made him want her more than all the others. Her blood seemed brighter, tasted sweeter.

The feeling was back.

As he finished, he thought she was almost gone. Haley's breathing had slowed.

He leaned over her and whispered in her ear. "I'm sorry."

<u>12</u>

"So Kinsinger is a fucking ghost? We really have nothing?" EP was pissed...frustrated.

"No, we got a lot," Kantz corrected his partner. "Just adds up to a whole lot of nothing. We're running on speculations. There are a lot of other candidates we should be looking at if you ask me." They had not asked him, he knew, but felt he was still allowed to theorize.

"Doesn't surprise me," Mahan was in early, put three coffees on EP's desk, and winked at him. "I had fun last night......again." She had brought over wine, three bottles, and EP had prepared a fresh spinach salad with a spicy French dressing and all the trimmings. He also pan seared two thick cut rib eye steaks on the stovetop citing that it was too hot to grill and two potatoes had been thrown into the microwave. Dinner had been delicious, the company better, and she had slept in his bed once again, and his pillows smelled of his cologne. She wanted to know what it was, but forgot to check the bathroom the following morning before she left. Kidder was interesting, different. He'd even made her wash the dishes.

"Me too."

"Am I missing something here?" Kantz raised an eyebrow, glared at EP in disbelief, yet curious. He then looked at Mahan, she didn't notice. Her ass was snug in a pair of tight jeans and her breasts tried to pop out of a tight fitting blue blouse. She was not wearing as much make-up as she normally did, and her hair was lazily thrown into a ponytail. Tuesday thought she looked tired, just how someone would look after a long night of sex. Coffee, no cosmetics, he figured it all added up. "Have I officially become the third wheel here?" And then there was her smile, he noticed. *Guilty.*

"It's not what you think." EP blushed. *Or is it?* He wondered.

"Whatever you say."

"Can we please focus on something important?" EP noticed Tuesday checking out Mahan's rear. He looked too, couldn't help himself. She saw them as well, and cleared her throat to startle them. *If he wanted to check out my ass, all he had to do was crawl in bed with me last night.*

"I'd say you boning the help is important Kidder. Lucky bastard."

"I'm standing right here." Mahan wasn't offended. She knew she had a nice ass.

"Jesus," EP tried not to laugh. "Do you always have to think like a pervert? Nobody's *boning* anybody."

"Again, whatever you say boss."

"What were you about to say?" EP said directly to Mahan. "What doesn't surprise you?"

"How small your pecker is!" Tuesday chuckled so hard his belly shook. There was always room for one more joke. They all laughed. "Please go on agent Pierce. I apologize."

"I was just going to say it doesn't surprise me that we haven't been able to find a lot of information on Kinsinger. *If* he's our man, he's been planning on these killings for a while, probably years before he actually struck the first time. Most serial killers are highly intelligent, and know how to stay off the radar of law enforcement. The randomness of the victims already puts us behind in the investigation. But beyond that, I'd bet he doesn't have a single credit card in his name, or cell phone. He wouldn't want to leave any paper trails."

"Well yeah, but we seriously got jack shit on this guy," Kantz sipped his coffee with a slurp. "You're right, there are no credit cards in his name, but there's also no utility bill addressed to him. Bastard has to live somewhere though. We know he's not homeless. There's no cable bill, zilch."

"And he hasn't changed his address since he moved. DMV has no record of him taking up residence anywhere else."

"Maybe he started killing right after he moved and that's why he doesn't want anyone to have a way of tracking him?" EP looked towards Kantz. "Let's start a timeline." Jimmy was ready for his orders. "Go back and see when was the last time Kinsinger lived at his last address and compare it to when the first victim was taken. See what turns up." Just like that, Kantz was gone. Kidder was back with Mahan, and he continued. "So how can one not exist? We know he works. We know that he has a car. He's got to live somewhere....."

"I'll get my people to do a background on any known family members of Kinsinger. Maybe some of them have multiple properties here that he's renting from or staying with? He could be hiding behind someone else's name?"

Kidder nodded. "What time is it?"

"A little after nine, why?"

"Let's go check on that tile job. I want to meet this asshole face to face. We got a lot of questions for Abraham Kinsinger."

*

Abraham knew they were coming.

Miguel had warned him and he swore he would not say anything. He would act surprised when they arrived. At least they would not be able to catch him by surprise. He had asked Miguel what type of questions they were asking, and he told him everything he knew. Now he had time to prepare for their questions, to rehearse his answers, and calm his nerves.

They were too close to him.

How the fuck did they know his name?

"I told them you were a good kid Abe. I told those assholes they were wasting their time, but they just wouldn't listen."

"It's okay," Abraham replied. "They're just doing their job."

*

Franklin Tidwell was horny.
His daughter was missing, yet he was aroused.
Molly would not have anything to do with him.
She was starting to get on his nerves anyway.
And she had lost her looks years ago.
Grabbing a towel, he left the hotel room at the Ramada and headed for the pool.
There were always girls at the pool.

*

"His name is Karl Avant." Henry Riker was a parole officer wanting to help. He'd been drinking buddies with Tuesday for years and Kantz had kept him up to speed with the investigation. "I'm telling you Jimmy. You should probably take a closer look at this guy."

"What makes you think it's him?"

"He's been keeping his appointments with me, but he seems just a little too interested in this case. He's asked me questions about it. He was convicted of raping three women twelve years ago. He was twenty-two at the time."

"How long has he been out? Have you paid him a visit?"

"He's been out about six years and yeah I've been to his house. I stop by there regularly. Something about this guy gives the creeps." The girls started disappearing six years ago. It fit the timeline.

"Always trust your gut," Kantz had learned the hard way. Ten years ago, when he was on patrol, he pulled over a large conversion van. The plates weren't registered to the vehicle, and as he approached the car, something told him to use caution. But there had been an elderly woman, in her seventies, behind the wheel, and he allowed his guard to slip. He had taken her license and walked away from the van, turning his back to the rear door. The next thing he remembered he was in the back of an ambulance in route to the hospital. Her grandson had been in the back of the van and had fired two rounds into Tuesday's back. They missed his spine by inches and landed in his abdomen. He barely survived that incident, and come to find out, the grandson had escaped from a work release program two weeks prior, and had enough drug money to flee the country. Grandma was taking him to the airport. The entire drug operation went through her home, using a child daycare as cover. "All right, I'll look into it. I'll add this piece of shit to the list."

"Good. They should've never let this guy out. I'm telling you, he's got issues. You got any other leads?"

"We got a list of names that's going to take the

rest of the year to go through. Kidder is gung ho about this one asshole. He's on his way to interview him now."

"He's trusting his gut on this one?"

"Yep." It amazed Kantz how everyone's instincts were different. "Poor bastard. He's good at detective work, puts in the hours, and keeps a cool head about him. But I'd sure hate to be in his shoes. Having to walk in his father and grandfather's footsteps and all."

"Ah, the Kidder legacy." Riker was aware of the family's history.

"Yeah, like I said," Kantz breathed heavily into the phone. "Poor bastard."

"Well keep me posted."

"I will. Thanks."

*

The neighborhood was nice, clean, and quiet.

Mr. Hampton's old Ford pick-up was parked in the driveway, and a gold Buick LeSabre was parked at the curb. It did not appear the homeowners were present. EP and Mahan parked behind the sedan and climbed out. They flanked each side of the car and peered inside. There was nothing out of the ordinary. The car was clean, *too clean*, EP thought. Mr. Hampton was in the back of his truck and noticed them right away. He met them at the foot of the driveway. "Is he here?" EP looked the man up and down, he knew Miguel did not care for him very much. That was okay with him.

"Yes, he's here," Miguel snarled. He was glad his clients were not home. He had a good reputation in St. Augustine, and was annoyed detectives were showing up at one of his jobsites. "Just like I said he'd be. He's inside ripping up linoleum in the master bathroom. We gotta have this job done in two days. I hope this won't take very long."

"Can you go get him please?"

Miguel grunted under his breath and turned to enter the home. But before he could make his way up the driveway, Abraham emerged through the garage with two armfuls of green and white checkered linoleum and slung it into the back of his boss's truck. "Done," he smiled and noticed the two detectives standing by his car at the end of the driveway. His smile wanted to fade, but he forced it to stay. *So these are the cocksuckers who think they're smarter than me?* He did want to meet them in a way; he had learned that Kidder was in charge of the task force trying to catch him through periodicals he had scanned on the internet. The Kidder name was always in the city's headlines, and he was familiar with them. He and Miguel had even done some work in a house owned by a relative of the Kidder dynasty. He had a lot of power, Abraham knew, and a lot of connections.

"Mr. Kinsinger," Mahan began and she watched as the man behind Miguel's truck started towards them. He was smiling, did not appear agitated, or alarmed. *Miguel must have warned him*, she knew but had no proof, never would. They finally stopped in the middle of the driveway and the three of them exchanged perceptual glances that seemed to last an eternity. "I'm special agent Pierce with the FBI." She showed him her credentials. "And this is Detective Kidder. We're sorry to bother you, but we have a few questions we need you to answer. Is that okay?"

Abraham extended his hand towards Kidder and nodded. They both gripped each other's hand firmly. Neither man wanted to back down from the other, but Abraham retreated first. "Detective Kidder," Abraham began, still smiling. "It's nice to meet you. I read about your family all the time. What is that they call you? The *Golden Boy*? They say you're going to run this town someday. I'd vote for you." Miguel had disappeared inside the house. His cheeks were hardened with anger. He wanted them to leave.

"I'm not on a political campaign Mr. Kinsinger." EP wanted him to stop smiling. It was not setting right with him. "We're here on a murder investigation and possible kidnapping." He waited for a reaction from Abraham. His smile faded, and his eyes took on a look of genuine concern. Not the reaction he was looking for.

"Murder? How could I possibly help you with that?"

"We need to know where you were on the night of July fourth." Mahan rushed the question, tried to send him reeling. "You're entitled to council during this questioning Mr. Kinsinger. But we really need you to clear a few things up." He waived his rights.

"At home." Abraham answered, he looked confused. "Why?"

"Can anyone vouch for your whereabouts? Was anyone with you?"

"No, no, I was alone. I keep to myself most of the time."

No alibi, EP thought silently. *Good.* "Where do you live anyway? You are a very hard man to track down."

"I live in an old house off Lewis Speedway. No big secret. It belongs to my uncle, Philip Foster. He lives in Atlanta, let's me stay there cheap. House is paid for, but he doesn't want to sell it. Hasn't been a very good housing market around here lately, I'm sure you're aware." He looked directly at Kidder, ignoring Mahan for the moment. He knew what they were going to ask next. "And if you're about to ask me about the utilities, or cable, those bills are in his name also. They've never been turned off. I personally go and pay them in cash every month."

"You don't even have a bank account. Doesn't that strike you as being rather odd?"

"Not really, I pay everything in cash. That's how Mr. Hampton pays me. I don't have a need for one. That's not a crime is it?"

"It's strange Mr. Kinsinger."

"Well, your last statement isn't entirely true either. I *do* have a trust fund in my name. When my mother passed away, she had a life insurance policy and I was listed as the beneficiary. I was only eleven back then though and it was put in a trust fund by my father. Wasn't allowed to touch it until I was twenty-five, but still haven't seen the need to mess with it. Hoping it's enough to retire on down the road though. I keep up with it online, through The Hartford, but the statements have been sent to my father since the fire............since my mother passed."

How had they missed the trust fund? "Where is your father?"

"Don't know. Haven't seen him, Henry, in years. He doesn't write, doesn't call. Just doesn't want to be a part of my life I guess. He left me and my mother when I was two. Never really knew him."

"What about when your mother died, who'd you stay with?"

"My uncle."

"Philip?"

Abraham nodded. "Man, you guys are good," he smiled again. "Always wondered what it would be like to chase bad guys. You guys good at it?" They did not have to answer, and chose not to. "I can tell you are. Still don't see what this has to do with me though?"

Mahan ignored him, she sensed his fascination with EP. *Why,* she wondered. "We're going to need your address Mr. Kinsinger and we'd like to take a look around your property if that's ok?" *I'm the one he'd rape and torture. Was he into men too?*

"Sure. It would be my pleasure." He looked back towards the house, searched for a sign of Miguel. "You guys want to follow me over there? Just let me go tell Mr. Hampton where we're going....."

"That won't be necessary," Kidder called Abraham back. "I'm sure he'll understand. And no point in all of us driving over there is there? We'd be more than happy to escort you. We'll bring you right back."

"I guess that's okay."

They started walking towards EP's unmarked car and Mahan opened the door for him. "Buckle up."

"Always do."

Then Kidder started in on him again as he stirred the engine. "Abraham, you seem like a bright guy. Are you aware it's against the law to fail notifying the state of Florida of any address changes? I believe you have twenty days after moving to notify the DMV and any other agencies of the address change. It's a misdemeanor in the state of Florida, and you could be sanctioned to a hefty fine. You wouldn't want that now would you?"

"No, I was not aware of that." Abraham lied, he knew the law. "And no I wouldn't want the fine. I'm sorry for the confusion. I'll take care of it right away."

"Why?" EP asked and eyeballed Abraham

through the rearview mirror. "You haven't changed it in almost 6 years. Why do it now?" The question was sarcastic, and Abraham chose not to answer this time. EP had not heard from Tuesday, but assumed that as soon as Abraham moved out of his apartment and into his uncle's house, the killings had begun, and Abraham had vanished from the realm of society at the same time. Still, as of right now, they had nothing. He knew that, and so did Abraham.

Perhaps, Abraham thought as he shifted uneasily in the backseat. *Perhaps I should get an attorney?*

"You okay back there?" Mahan looked at the sketch in her hand and peered behind the seat at Abraham.

"I'm fine."

"Do you think you look like this man?"

Abraham took the sketch and stared at it. There were similarities, but not many. He'd already seen it a dozen times on the television. "No," he answered. "That's not me."

"What if I told you we had a couple of witnesses that saw you leaving the parking lot of the Ramada Inn on the night of July fourth pulling a large suitcase behind you?"

"I'd say they were mistaken. I wasn't there." *How do they know that? Goddamnit!*

"And if I told you about the clerk that might be able to identify you?"

"Listen, I'm willing to cooperate with you anyway I can." He handed the sketch back to Mahan. "But this is not me. I don't have anything to hide."

"Then you wouldn't mind coming down to the station to stand in a lineup?"

"Do cops really still do that?" he asked, and laughed coldly. "I thought that only happened on television."

"So?"

"If it clears me, sure. I guess I'll do it." The car turned onto Lewis Speedway. They were almost to his house. "But if it's okay with you, I think I've changed my mind."

"About what?" EP questioned, his eyes fixed on the winding road.

"I think I will exercise my right to an attorney."

"That's probably a good idea Mr. Kinsinger."

"Make your next left."

*

Tuesday found Karl at his home, working underneath the hood of a rusty old blue Chevy Corvette, one from the Stingray series. He was a burly man, wore a blue shirt with holey jeans. A cigarette hung from a set of stained teeth, and he hadn't shaved in days. Kantz knew the feeling. "Trying to bring *her* back to life?" He asked referring to the car.

"Bitch is more trouble than she's worth if you ask me." Karl looked up and saw the badge and gun hanging from Jimmy's waistline. He spit out the cigarette and drove it into the dirt with the heel of his boot. "What's your business here? I ain't violated my parole."

"You heard about that girl that went missing?"

"Sure. It's all over the news. But I didn't have anything to do with that."

"Where were you on the night of the fourth?"

"Here...at home."

"Were you alone?"

"No."

"Mind telling me who you were with?"

Karl was silent. "Man look, I don't want to get in no trouble. I've served my time."

"I'm not here to bust your chops Karl. Just answer the question."

"I was with a woman."

"Girlfriend?"

"No."

"Prostitute?" If he were, it would mean he violated his probation. He promised if his story panned out, he would let it slide. "You got my word. But I need her name and I'm gone."

"Her name is Cookie, least that's what they call her on the street."

"Ah shit, I know Cookie," Kantz laughed and turned away from Karl. "She shouldn't be too hard to find. Good luck with your Stingray. Don't go skipping town on me now. I may be back."

"Can't wait." *Damn cops.*

*

The house was old, and hidden off a dangerous curve on Lewis Speedway. The roof was in dire need of repair, and old white paint curled and chipped around the entire exterior of the home. Surrounded by a bundle of overgrown bushes and trees, the entire property was isolated by forestry. You couldn't see the house from the road. And there were separated patches of grass, but dirt made up the majority of the compound. Trees blocked most of the sunlight.

Mahan looked around.

It was quiet.

"Please, come inside." Abraham opened the door and they followed him in. Directly through the front door was an oversized living room and the kitchen was immediately to the right. It was clean, floors smelled of pine-sol and bleach. Two couches sat along the left wall of the living room, with a single coffee table in front, and a small television set sat across from it on the right side wall. Mahan walked into the kitchen and looked around while EP started to follow Abraham through the rest of the house.

Mahan opened the fridge and peered inside. Save for a half gallon of milk, a few LunchAble's and a carton of eggs, it was empty. Freezer had a few Hungry-Man frozen dinners and couple trays of ice. Nothing out of the ordinary. Then she opened the cabinet underneath the sink and found a bunch of household cleaning supplies. She saw the pine-sol her nose detected, and the bleach. The bleach was sitting next to a bottle of acetone. The acetone was out of place, she thought, and then turned to catch up with the two men.

EP entered the first bedroom on the left.

It was simple.

There was a nightstand with a lamp next to a bed.

And that was it.

No sheets were on the bed. EP thought that was odd. "Where are the bed sheets?"

"Don't need any," Abraham offered an explanation. "I live alone. If I ever have company, I'll pull some out." Abraham lied. He'd washed them, and stored them in the closet. He'd put the audio and video monitors and the shackles in a box up in the attic as well. The bedroom had been thoroughly cleaned. He was sure he'd thought of everything.

EP left the room as Mahan entered. Abraham followed him to his bedroom.

Mahan looked briefly around the room, and

saw nothing at first. Then, she walked around to the end of the bed and pulled the mattress from against the wall. She looked down the side of the bed. Nothing. She put the mattress back and was about to exit the room when she saw something on the leg of the bed frame.

Scuff marks??

It looked like something had been attached to the metal.

Handcuffs? A chain?

She couldn't be sure.

The rest of their visit went quickly.

EP asked Abraham if he owned any suitcases. Abraham showed them his luggage. All of them were far too small to transport a body. He'd hidden the suitcase in question in the attic as well, under a pile of insulation. He planned on retrieving everything later, and disposing of it properly.

The drive back to Abraham's jobsite was silent.

All three of them were processing information. *Had they found something?* Abraham wondered. If so, they were being tight-lipped about it. *Should I say something? No. Just keep your damn mouth shut.*

"Thanks for the lift," Abraham nodded towards them as he climbed out of the car.

"We'll be in touch Mr. Kinsinger. Thanks for your cooperation." Mahan offered a smile, though she did not mean it.

"Looking forward to it."

They watched him disappear back inside the house; Miguel had met him in the garage. As they left, Mahan started in. "We have to get a warrant and get back in that house. It was too clean. The bleach smell was too distinct. And the mattress looked scrubbed. The absence of sheets troubles me."

"Me too."

"And it may not mean anything, but he had bleach and acetone under the sink in the kitchen." EP did not understand. "Those are the ingredients to make homemade chloroform," she informed him. "And I can't be sure without further tests, but one of the legs of the bed frame had scuff marks on them. I'm thinking someone may have been chained to the bed......."

"Going to be hard to prove."

"Yes, but do you know an easy judge? All we have is a theory based on circumstantial evidence, but surely we have enough for a warrant? Got anybody in mind?"

Kidder did not know a judge off hand, but he knew who to call.

"I'll call my father."

*

Abraham worked the rest of the day in deep thought. He had assured Miguel that everything was fine, yet he was not so sure. They knew his name, and something had brought them to his doorstep? And what about the people that could identify him? What was he going to do about that? He did not want to go through a line-up, wouldn't.

EP was tough, he could tell. He was not going to go away or back off.

And Mahan was smart, like him. She looked at things *differently*, and he figured neither of them believed a word he said. She had also spent a lot of time in the spare bedroom. *Why?* He quizzed. *She'd seen something*, he was sure.

That meant they would be coming back.

He had to get rid of the bed.

I'll take care of it when I get home.
Then he thought about Haley Tidwell.
And that foreign feeling returned.
He missed her……….

<u>13</u>

"Give me some time and I'll get you a warrant." Stephen Kidder wanted this to end just as bad as his son. "In the meantime, send over everything you've got on Kinsinger. Judge Ramsey is an old college friend. He'll help us."

"Thanks," EP hung up and turned to Mahan. He waited for her to finish her conversation, watched her lips move. "Got anything else?"

"There are a lot of people that fit our profile," she looked flustered. "But if it's Kinsinger, I don't want to waste anymore time chasing down other leads."

"It's him. It's got to be."

"I think we should talk to the uncle, Philip Foster."

"Want me to track him down?"

"Already done." Mahan had connections too…the federal government. "You can give me a lift to the airport though. I want to talk to Foster in person."

"You're going to Atlanta?"

"Yeah, but I'll be back tonight. Can you pick me up?"

"Sure. I'll try to track down the father, Henry Kinsinger, while you're gone."

"Thanks. Keep my bed warm."

"You know, my neck hurts from sleeping on the couch."

"I'm sorry."

"Are you?"

She was, and she had no problem showing him.

*

Abraham worked fast.

He had borrowed Miguel's truck, and loaded the mattress, box spring, and frame in the bed of the truck. He'd promised to return the truck by evening, telling Miguel he needed the truck to help a friend move. Then, he drove to what was normally a deserted canal entrance and looked around. No one was there.

He had to move.

He waded waist high into the water and threw the metal bed frame into the murky channel.

Once back at the truck, he lifted the box spring and mattress out of the back and found a good spot on the ground. He went back for the gasoline container and doused the bed with fuel. He fumbled with a few matches, struggling with the ocean breeze, but finally got one lit.

He watched the bed burn for a few minutes.

There was nothing left except the metal springs.

But there had been a lot of smoke. He hoped no one had seen anything, and did not want to hang around to find out.

He took a moment to change his pants, and threw his wet pair into the canal before driving away.

No one passed him on the way out.

No one had seen anything.

Abraham Kinsinger turned on the radio and could not wait to get his car back. He craved a cigarette.

Miguel did not smoke.

He knew there was something about Miguel Hampton he did not like.

*

Mahan arrived in Atlanta as scheduled at five o'clock in the evening. The bureau had a car waiting for her at Hartsfield International Airport, and an agent in the area had already contacted Philip Foster and requested a meeting between the two. He had agreed, and they met at a restaurant, an Applebee's, just off the turnpike from the airport. He was an architect and his office was close by. He lived in Marietta, about an hours drive from the airport in traffic, and Mahan wanted to be closer to the airport.

"Thanks for meeting me on such short notice."

"Sure, no problem." Philip was a small man, almost sixty, very small and out of shape. He had brown hair laced with gray. He was clean shaven, but his face was plump. He wore a pair of round, thick coke-bottle glasses and his eyes were dark and sad. "Agent I spoke with said you needed to ask me some questions pertaining to an ongoing investigation?" He looked shocked. Had no idea what was going on, but seemed eager enough to help. Either that or he wanted attention. His ring finger was naked. *No wife*, Mahan thought. *Perhaps no one to talk to at home?* "Can't say I remember a time when an FBI agent wanted to question me."

"That's a good thing," Mahan smiled. He seemed harmless. She sensed he would help her, if he could. They ordered drinks and an appetizer, she settled for shrimp skewers. She wanted more crab claws, but they weren't listed on the menu. She missed St. Augustine, she thought, surprisingly. "Okay," she continued once they were both settled. "I guess I'll just jump right into it." Philip nodded. "It's about your nephew, Abraham Kinsinger."

Foster looked puzzled. "Abe," he said. "Has

something happened to him? Poor boy's been through so much......"

"He's fine," Mahan charged forward. Better to get to the point. "But he's become a person of interest in an investigation." Philip leaned in, his ears twitched. He was involved. "A murder investigation Mr. Foster, the kidnapping and murder of what we now believe to be six women..........possibly more."

"I'm afraid I don't understand. I can't imagine he'd be involved in anything like that Agent Pierce. It just boggles my mind."

"Are you close to him?"

"Not really, maybe talk to him once or twice a year. I've only seen him once since he moved into my house in St. Augustine six years ago. He pays the bills, does things, and fixes things around there to help me out. He's good at fixing things. Anyway, I was in town to take care of a few things, visit a few other relatives in Jacksonville and thought I'd stop by to check on him, and the house."

"Did he seem happy to see you?"

"Couldn't tell. He doesn't have a phone, so I surprised him I guess."

"When was this?"

"Couple of summer's ago."

"After July Fourth?"

"Yeah. Actually it was in September. I remember because I had to drive through a wave of those darn love bugs. Did you know they come out from the ground twice a year? Once in May, and again in September I believe. Can't be sure. But I was there definitely a couple of years ago in September."

"Did you notice anything out of the ordinary?"

"No," Philip sipped his drink. "House was clean, Abraham seemed fine. I slept on the couch that night. We had dinner, got caught up. He seemed fine."

Must've already dumped the body, Mahan thought. "Is there anything at all you can tell me about him, about his childhood that might help me? We want to exclude him as a suspect if we can. But there's a lot of things that are making us feel uneasy. If you can tell me anything at all, it would really be a big help."

"I'm not sure what you want to know Agent Pierce. Abe's father, Henry Kinsinger, was a sorry piece of shit. Don't think he ever really cared for my sister, or Abe. He walked out on them when Abe was two. My sister was never really the same after that. Don't think she ever got over it. Tell you the truth, I've always kind of blamed Henry for her death. She became depressed, started drinking, lost interest in her life as a whole. As soon as he left her, it seemed as though everything just started crumbling. Just a bad situation…up until the night she died…"

"Can you tell me about that?" Mahan wasn't afraid to ask tough questions. "I know it's difficult, but it could be important."

"What do you want to know?"

"What happened that night?"

"Just a tragedy. According to the investigators, Helena had been drinking heavily. She simply passed out in bed with a lit cigarette and never woke up. I don't think she had a chance to escape."

"Was Abraham there at the time?"

"Yeah, I think he was around eleven years old when it happened. He woke up to the fire, ran to a neighbor's house and they called 911. By the time the firemen got there, well it was too late, there wasn't much left of the house."

"And you took Abraham in?"

"Yeah, Henry was nowhere to be found. He came around from time to time, but made it clear he didn't want to have anything to do with him. Think he just wanted to sell the property, cash in the check if you know what I mean? I really don't like him Agent Pierce. Have you met him yet?"

Mahan shook her head. "How long did he live with you?"

"Until he was twenty. I bought him a car, a gold Buick for his birthday. I think he still drives it for that matter. I know I saw it in the driveway the last time I visited."

"Where'd he go then?"

"Back to St. Augustine. Stayed with a couple of cousins for a while, until he found a job and got on his feet. Then he moved out on his own somewhere. Not real sure where. Thought he had intentions of going to school, but I guess it never panned out. That's a shame really. He's a very intelligent person. Read more books than anyone I've ever met."

"What kind of books?"

"All of them, anything he could get his hands on." He paused to order another drink. Mahan checked her watch. She had to leave soon. "Is any of this helping?" Philip wondered. "I can't imagine going through what that poor kid has been through. Growing up without a father would be hard enough, but then watching your mother die in a fire…..I just can't imagine. Overall, I think he's held it together pretty good. I did the best I could with him, honest."

"I believe you, and yes, you've been a big help. Sorry to intrude your life so suddenly." She finished her drink and prepared to leave. She'd be back in St. Augustine no later than eight o'clock, she thought, and then wondered what EP was going to cook for her tonight? She also wondered if he was going to crawl in the bed with her. "Thanks again." She got up, hardly touched the shrimp. "If I need anything else, may I call you?"

"Certainly."

She started to walk away, but Philip called her name. "Yes Mr. Foster. Is there something else?"

"I'm not sure, could be nothing."

"Go on," Mahan felt he was about to share something important. "We need to help Abraham if we can. I can't know if he's involved or not unless I know everything. You can trust me Mr. Foster."

"It's nothing really," Philip reluctantly continued. He didn't want to sound stupid. He was not a detective. "I was just curious about what you asked me earlier. When I mentioned that I had gone to visit him a couple of years ago, you asked me if it was after July Fourth."

"Yes. Does that mean something to you?"

"Not sure. Just curious as to why that particular date is important?"

"What is it you want to tell me?"

"It's just strange you asked that."

"How so?"

"Because now that I'm thinking about it, I'm pretty sure that it was around the Fourth of July when his father walked out on him and my sister….."

"Interesting."

"And," he continued. Mahan did not realize he had more to add. She couldn't believe what she heard next. "This is all very surreal, and I can't be a hundred percent right now, but I'm also almost certain that the night of the fire….the night my sister died……"

"Yes. Mr. Foster, what is it?"

"I think that also happened on the Fourth of July. I know I said I'm not sure, but I am. I'm certain. I'm sure."

Mahan turned and walked away but muffled something under her breath…..*Holy Shit!*

14

Abraham had dinner with Miguel after he returned the truck. It was not planned, but his boss had offered and he knew it would be impolite to refuse. He had to act normal, could not show things were bothering him. He felt the walls of his world collapsing around him. He could still feel eyes watching him. *They knew*, he thought. *They knew the truth about him, who he really was. And they had witnesses, wanted to put him in a line-up.* "The stroganoff was excellent, thank you." He tried to show nothing was wrong.

"You sure you okay?"

"Yeah."

"We should do this more often Abe." Miguel sensed a tension had fallen over them. "I've come to rather enjoy your company." Abraham got up to leave, offered to help Miguel with the cleanup. His offer was declined. "Nonsense. Go home. I can take care of this. I'm old but I can still function. Let me know if you need anything. I'm here for you."

"Thank you."

Abraham should have said *goodbye*. He knew he would never see him again.

He also should have gone home at this point, but did not.

A quick trip to the Ramada won't hurt anything...

He could not control himself..........and was going in that direction anyway.

Once on San Marco, he was forced to stop at a red light. He could see the hotel and a few restaurants in the distance. When the light turned green, he continued on his way, drumming the steering wheel with his fingers, and humming a tune he could not name. The Ramada was on his left, and he passed it, and then hung a right into the nearest restaurant. The parking lot was crowded. *Perfect.* He knew no one would pay him any attention and parked in the back.

He walked inside the restaurant; it was new to the area, more of a bar than anything else, called the Pink Flamingo. A hostess offered to seat him, and he declined. He only wanted to place an order to go.

He ordered twenty hot chicken wings, and an order of curly fries. The celery and carrots were complimentary, he was told.

While he waited, he looked in the merchandise case.

A Pink Flamingo shirt was fifteen bucks.

A hat of matching color went for ten.

Abraham purchased both and also paid for the food in cash.

What are you doing? He asked himself as he changed clothes in the backseat of his car. *Just go home.*

He could not.

Abraham swiftly crossed the street, careful to stay hidden in the shadows as best he could. The streetlights of St. Augustine were dim anyway, and he found himself in the Ramada parking lot less than a minute later. He walked around the lobby, was sure the camera's had been turned back on, but had his Pink Flamingo hat pulled low. He never looked up towards the cameras as he climbed the set of stairs.

He did not have too. He knew exactly where he was going.

Without hesitation, he knocked on the door. It took a few seconds but a woman answered.

Molly Tidwell, he thought. *Haley's mother.*

"Can I help you?" Her voice was soft and tired. He wondered what was going through her head. She had no idea she was standing face to face with the man that had taken her daughter. She wasn't alarmed though, his disguise and the smell of the food worked. She looked weak, weary. As she spoke again, he noticed the similarities between mother and daughter and he fought hard to subdue his excitement. The itch was back. "You must have the wrong room." She noticed the food, assumed the delivery was a mistake.

"You sure?" Abraham really wanted to get inside the room. He could have forced his way inside at that moment, but did not. *Control yourself asshole.* "Says here delivery to room 206 at the Ramada. Tidwell? Is that you?"

"Well yes, that is me, but I swear I haven't ordered any food." She still did not look concerned, or angry.

"Is there anyone else that could have ordered it?"

"I guess my husband could have, but he's not here. He's in the sports bar downstairs. Been there all afternoon. Suits me." She offered this information freely. She honestly hoped Frank would return drunk enough to fall over. "Why don't you check down there? I'm sorry for the trouble."

"No trouble at all. Have a good night Mrs. Tidwell."

And he left.

Good boy.

Before he entered the bar, he threw the food in a nearby trash can.

He found Frank sitting alone at a table near the corner.

The place was busy for a weeknight.

A college game screamed through three flat screen televisions, but he paid no attention to who was playing. He nudged his way through the crowd and passed Franklin Tidwell on his way to the bathroom. He didn't have to go; he just wanted to see what he was drinking. Looked like whiskey and coke. When he came out of the bathroom, a waitress was with Frank. He was ordering another drink.

"Make that two," Abraham smiled and the waitress took off. "Mind if I sit," he turned his attention to Frank. "Place is crowded. No room at the bar."

"Free country." Frank was drunk.

"Thanks. You from here?" No words, Franklin just shook his head. "I am. Cool place to visit but I don't suggest living here." The waitress returned with their drinks and walked away shaking her hips from side to side. Her shorts were too short. Abraham noticed the oval of her vagina. He knew Franklin saw it too, had probably been looking at it all night. "However, there are a lot of good looking beach bunnies around here. I'm sure you've seen them."

Franklin smiled.

He thought about his wife, Molly.

Then his daughter.

Fuck em, he thought nastily and gazed towards the waitress. He looked her up and down.

He wanted her.

Abraham saw it in his eyes.

And wanted to kill him.

"You're a good looking kid, bet you've been lucky enough to score with an assortment of these delicacies huh?" *Delicacies? Is that what you call them? Is that how you see your daughter...I did.* "It's okay friend. You can be honest with me. If you've seen my wife, you'd know why I'm so curious, why I'm sitting in this bar alone instead of having my hot air balloon of a wife ruin my enjoyment of the eye candy around here." *I have seen her…almost killed her just a few minutes ago.* Abraham wanted to tell him everything. "Seriously, how many?"

"Too many to count," Abraham finally spoke aloud, slugged his drink. "But I remember *all* of them." He did.

"Know any that might be interested in an old geezer like me?"

Abraham wanted to make Frank angry. Wanted to see that side of him. "How much money do you have?" Frank's smile faded and his lips curled. He stared at Abraham for a moment, and for a second, he thought he was about to lunge at him from across the small table. *Come on,* Abraham smiled. *Do it mother fucker! DO IT!*

Franklin Tidwell remained composed, however. He thought before he spoke, and smiled. "Are you suggesting that I'm so ugly that I have pay for the finer things in life?" He referred to women, and his daughter. "I think you got me all wrong friend. I do okay. I can get what I want."

"I wasn't trying to offend you." *Yes I was.*
"You didn't." *Yes I did.*
"I was just saying, I know some girls that will do anything for *coke*." Abraham had never done cocaine, never would, but continued with the sincerity of the Pope. "You score some powder and they'll do anything you want for as long as you want. You into that?"

"Not since college."
"Ah, never mind then."
"Not saying I wouldn't. When can you make

this happen?"

"How long you in town for?"

"Couple more days."

"That's more than enough time. Why don't you give me your number and I'll call you in a day or two." Abraham remained calm, but was pissed. *Fucker isn't even worried about his daughter. I should tell him everything. I should tell him he'll never see his daughter again. I should tell him that I was the last person that would enjoy her, taste her. That would piss him off....*

"What's in it for you?" Frank was a little skeptical, and hesitant to give out his cell number.

"A good time. I need you to pay for the *dust*. I don't have a lot of money." He pointed to his hat and shirt. "I'm a fucking dishwasher at the Pink Flamingo." To him, lying was an art form, like a Picasso, only he did not have to use as many strokes to get people to see his *painting*.

At first, he thought Frank was going to change his mind. He'd be smart too. But he did not know what he was capable of, what he had done, or what he was going to do. And he knew the thought of young *tenderloin* would be too hard to pass up. In the end, he wrote his number down and handed it to Abraham.

"Franklin Tidwell," he said introducing himself.

"Nice to meet you Frank," Abe shook his hand. The grip was firm, challenging. *Bring it on mother fucker.* "I'm Angelo Richards."

"Angelo? That's a weird name."

It was, but flip it around and you got Richard Angelo, a famous serial killer known as the *Angel of Death*. Abraham amused himself every time he used what he thought were historical references. *I wonder what they'll call me.* He wanted a nickname, felt he deserved one, definitely earned it. "Yeah, but it gets me what I want, what we both want."

"And what's that?" Frank knew the answer.

"Pussy."

And then Abraham promised to call, soon, and left before he got blood on his hands.

*

EP fried crab-claws, even concocted his own batter, a blend of flour, salt, pepper, a dab of Worcestershire sauce for kick, and dash of cayenne pepper for oomph. He melted a stick of butter, and added a generous helping of garlic salt for dipping. He didn't cook anything else. He didn't need too, but did have a bag of tortilla chips and salsa for easy added pleasure. If this did not impress Mahan, he had already impressed himself. *She still better like it*, he thought and sipped his wine.

"Delicious," Mahan said, very impressed. "Fuck Fiddler's Green. When I want crab-claws, I'm going to fuckin' Kidder's Kitchen." She laughed, ate some more, a lot more, and enjoyed more wine. EP was curious about Atlanta and she gave him the scoop on what Philip Foster had shared with her.

"No shit." EP wanted to go to Kinsinger's house that instant, wanted to kick his ass. "So we got six missing girls, all on the Fourth of July, and we got two tragic events in Kinsinger's life, both on the Fourth of July?"

"Yep," Mahan chugged the bottom half of her glass of wine and poured some more. *Would tonight be the night*, she wondered, wanted. "God bless America."

"Your profile was right on." EP was turned on.

"Yeah, but we still have to catch him."

"We'll get him." EP was certain. "He's our guy." He walked out onto his back deck, just as his father would although he did not notice the similarity, and phoned Kantz. He told him to stop rifling through other suspects, wanted *all* their efforts pointed at Abraham Kinsinger.

"You sure?" Tuesday was not.

"Have a drink Jimmy," EP wanted another one himself. He told him about what Mahan had found out from the uncle in Atlanta. He still wanted to talk to the father, Henry Kinsinger. "We'll probably have a warrant in the morning. I want to ring this asshole's neck."

"Not if I do it first." Tuesday jumped on the bandwagon. "Got a question though."

"Go ahead."

"Why is agent Pierce at your house again? It's after ten o'clock. Please tell me Kidder. My lips are sealed, I swear." He'd already poured a drink. "Can I come over?"

"Fuck off Jimmy," EP said, and hung up.

He walked back in the kitchen, and looked for Mahan. She wasn't there. The dishes were done and put away; he heard the soft drumming of his dishwasher. She wasn't in the living room either, or the bathroom.

He found her in his bedroom, again, under the covers, lying on her side so that her bare back faced him.

She took off her shirt. Had she done that before?

EP was about to enter the room when his cell phone rang.

"Ignore it," Mahan called from the bedroom. "It's been a long day. Whatever it is can wait until tomorrow."

It was his father, Stephen Kidder, it could not wait.

"Go ahead," he answered and closed the bedroom door behind him.

"I got it son," his father sounded lively for the time of night. "Get your ass out of bed. Call Mahan and Tuesday. I already got a half dozen uniforms and forensics waiting for you at the station."

"What's going on?"

"I got your warrant."

*

Abraham was not home an hour later.

EP felt he was not coming back. "We spooked him," he said to Mahan and gulped a cup of coffee. Neither one of them should have been driving in their condition. And if it were ever known that they were under the influence, he knew their *entire* investigation would go to shit. But EP had to be there, had to see this through to the end. He had to be the one to kick down the door.

"You don't think he's coming back?" Mahan chewed three pieces of gum. She also knew what was at stake. Both of them hesitated as they prepared to enter the house.

"Do you?"

Before she could answer, a member of the forensics team strolled outside, looked confused. Something was wrong. "What is it?"

"Warrant specifically listed the bed, frame, and all contents from the spare bedroom on the left in the hallway."

"Yeah...so?" EP already began walking inside, the person from forensics followed.

"Well, there's nothing in there. It's empty."

"No way," Mahan surged past both of them and walked into the bedroom where she'd seen scuff marks on the metal frame of the bed. It was not there. Nothing was there. The room was completely empty, and smelled of bleach and other cleaning supplies. She looked at EP, concerned. "He knew we were coming back. He knew we found something."

"This guy is fucking smart."

"I don't have a good feeling about this." Mahan exited the bedroom, went into the kitchen and opened up the cabinets beneath the sink, looking for the bleach and acetone, the stuff she suspected Abraham used to make chloroform. She paused, checked again, and then sighed and closed the cabinets. They were gone too. Abraham had taken them with him. "This is not good." EP was behind her, listening. "This is not good and all."

"The bleach and acetone are gone too?" Mahan answered with a nod, then opened the cabinets again, to be extra sure. She simply did not want to believe it. "Mahan, what does this mean?"

"It means he's changed. He's adapting to the situation, to us."

"I don't understand."

"I have to change my profile, there's only one reason he would do all this. He's probably destroyed *every* piece of evidence in this place, and there's only one reason he'd take the bleach and acetone….."

"To make more chloroform?"

"Yeah. But that's not it." She turned and looked into his eyes. This case was starting to get to her too. They must have rattled Abraham's cage, she knew, had gotten too close, and perhaps pushed him too far too soon. She should have suspected this would happen, if he felt threatened. She just didn't want to believe it. *Off my game.* "He's going to kill again EP." She felt helpless. Beaten. "Only this time, he's not going to wait until next Fourth of July!"

*

A lot of people went camping in Florida in the summer.
And Abraham knew where.
He did not want to do this, but had no choice. Eyes were watching him, *they* were coming for him, fuckin' Kidder and that cunt from the FBI knew his name. And they would catch him if he stayed.
That was not an option.
He was better than everyone he'd read about. To hell with Bundy, and Ridgeway. *Fuck'em all!*
He was number one!
Numero Uno!
He parked his car on the shoulder a good ways down the road; he did not want anyone to see his headlights.
And then he began walking quietly, but with a purpose, through the woods.....

*

Barry and Savannah were in love.
And they were too into each other's physical attributes to see Abraham coming.
Barry got on top of her, just as Abraham came up behind him.
He cut his throat with nothing more than the light of the campfire to guide him.
Savannah screamed at the sight of blood. The blade glistened in the moonlight. Though, she screamed only once.

The knife pierced her throat just as quickly as it had Barry's.

And Abraham thought about doing things to her, like he had all the others.

But he couldn't. He did not have that much time.

He jogged steadily back to his car satisfied they were dead and drove his gold Buick LeSabre to the campsite. He drug the bodies to his car and threw them inside, like rag dolls.

He searched the boy's pocket for the keys to the Honda CRV.

They were not there.

Must be the bitches car, he thought. *Should've known.*

He found the keys in her purse, and then threw the purse in his car as well. He started the engine of the CRV, just to make sure he could leave. He grabbed his clothes, the knife, the bleach and acetone, his smokes, everything he would need from his car and put them in the Honda. Then, he pulled more gasoline from his trunk and started dousing both the interior and exterior of his car. Using a log from the campfire, he set the Buick ablaze. He paused for a moment, just to watch what the heat and waves of flame did to human flesh. He thought about his mother, Helena, and the smell of her flesh as it started to burn that night....

Finally, satisfied, he climbed into the CRV and drove away.

He lit a cigarette and dropped the window.

He had to roll it down manually, aggravating.

But the fresh air did him some good.

He found a handgun in the glove box and smiled. It was a Ruger, 9mm, stainless steel with a black grip. Was not the gun he would have preferred,

but it would do.
 Lady luck…………...he thought…………It's my lucky fucking day.
 Then he pulled into the parking lot of the first convenient store he came to, walked inside, smelling of smoke and sweat, and casually bought a couple scratch off lottery tickets.
 I'll be damned, he said after using a dime to rub them in the car.
 And then walked back inside and collected $200.00 dollars.

15

Life was different after my mother died, after I killed her.

I was never worried about getting caught, I was a smart lil' fucker for eleven years old, even smarter now of course, but the fire had been a success. Newspapers wrote the story I told, Helena Kinsinger had died in an accidental fire, she had fallen asleep with a lit cigarette and the rest was history. Later, I learned that if I had used some type of accelerant, such as gasoline or lighter fluid, the arson investigators would have been able to detect the chemicals. Again, I was smart for eleven years old.

I remember feeling strange afterwards. Not guilt, or remorse of course, but strange that I didn't miss her.

Why would I?

And I was a little disappointed my father didn't come back into the picture after that, but he didn't. He'd reached an agreement with my uncle in Atlanta, my mom's brother, and I was shipped there for a few years. I felt like a package coming from one of those stupid home shopping network channels, what do they call that shit....QVC? I was thankful though because I blamed my father for everything. If he wouldn't have left us, my mother would have never started drinking, she would have never started touching me, and I probably would have never had to kill her. I convinced myself that Atlanta was for the best, for everybody, especially my father, because I'm certain that I would have eventually killed that bastard too.

Probably still will…..one day.

Atlanta was good for a while, I found peace, but

I knew it wouldn't last. Too many bad things had happened to me, and I had done too many bad things to get where I was. And no matter how hard I tried, and I did, I could never forget.

Those thoughts stayed with me, inside my head, eating away at my contrived sense of right and wrong.

I still don't think I know the difference.

Or just don't care.

I know I don't give a fuck.

I held a knife to my Uncle Philip's throat many times while he slept. I watched the rhythmic beating of his chest go up and down, up and down, up and fucking down. He woke up a few times, groggy, with blurred vision, and wanted to know what I was doing in his room, asked if anything was wrong. But it was dark and I just hid the knife behind my back and told him I couldn't sleep, that I was having nightmares about my mother's death…murder. And that always worked, the nightmare bullshit. I never had any, and he'd offer to let me crawl in bed with him sometimes. And I would from time to time, until I got older and it just seemed too weird. He never tried to touch me like Helena had, if he had, I would have killed him too. Luckily for him, that never happened, and I'd just lay there, from time to time, and watch him sleep, watch his chest go up and down…up and down.

I lived with him until my twentieth birthday.

I didn't have any friends, never even tried to make any, and my uncle Philip thought that was a little weird and unhealthy. Looking back, I think he was right, but I also don't think having friends would have stopped me from doing the things I would eventually do.

He even suggested therapy.

I refused, probably shouldn't have, but knew that shit wouldn't work either.

All I needed was my father's dirty magazines,

which I still had, still have, and when I moved back home to St. Augustine, I had accumulated a lot more, A LOT more material. My collection was awesome, but I'm pretty sure now those magazines weren't good for me. They kept images of my mother in my head, kept the evil inside me growing, until one day, those magazines simply weren't enough.

> *I was left alone in a society that failed me.*
> *And no one was around to watch over me.*
> *No one cared.*
> *I didn't exist, and that was okay with me.*
> *I was fucked up.*
> *And guess what, I still am.*
> *KILL...KILL...KILL...HAHAHAHAHAHA!*

*

"Connected with Henry Kinsinger," Tuesday informed EP from his desk working on his seventh cup of coffee. "Lives in Mobile, Alabama. On his fourth fucking marriage. Never understood why men do that shit. I've been married twice. Shit isn't for everybody. I know I'm not good at it, and would *never* do it again. No way."

"Get anything from him?" EP was on his way back to Miguel Hampton's shop. He had phoned ahead, and Miguel had agreed to meet him there directly. Though he had already been told that Abraham did not show up for work that morning and he had figured as much.

"Not a thing. Says he can't even remember the last time he talked to his son. He sounds like a piece of shit Kidder, honestly. And if you ask me, I think he was high on something. What kind of fuckin' asshole doesn't want to be a part of their son's life? Isn't that part of the obligation, especially when the other parent goes up in flames? Where's the father-son bond?"

"Will he travel down here?"

"Doesn't want to, but said he will if it's absolutely necessary. I don't think that ass-clown will be of any help though."

"No, tell him to make the damn trip." EP pulled into a Starbucks and ordered a coffee, grandee, no cream or sugar. Dark rings hung below his eyes, and he was tired but still kicking. He and Mahan had spent the night in Abraham's house and found nothing of any importance. "After everything that's happened, it's the least he can do. Besides, Kantz, we might need that ass-clown."

"Okay, I'll call him back right now. This should be fun…"

"You can handle it Jimmy, and if he doesn't want to cooperate, give the Mobile PD a call, tell them to put a foot in his ass."

"Roger that."

The call ended just as Mahan vibrated through. She didn't wait for "hello." "He drained his fucking trust fund," she said, coldly, emphatically, and hissed like a snake. "We're a day too late."

"How much?"

"Ninety thousand dollars."

"This guy is going to try and disappear."

"That's what I'm afraid of," Mahan agreed. They had played their hand all wrong, they should not have approached Abraham when they did, she knew now. Surveillance would have been the way to go, built a strong case, and then moved in when he wasn't looking. But he had seen them coming, and now they had to pay for it, work even harder. "I put a BOLO out on his Buick though. Got every cop in the state of Florida looking for it, along with Georgia and

Alabama."

"If he's still driving it, we'll find it." Kidder was not too sure of that.

"What about the father?" Mahan needed to change the subject.

"Henry Kinsinger lives in Mobile. We got in touch with him and I think he's agreed to come down."

"You think?"

"He'll get here, one way or another. It's a shame, really."

"What's that?"

"He's probably the one fucking person that could have put a stop to this. If he had just been a *father*, loved his son, maybe none of this would have happened. I doubt the stupid asshole even realizes it."

"They never do, but that's not a crime."

"It should be."

*

Mahan played everything in her head.

All their evidence was circumstantial, every bit.

They had no body, or *bodies*. And from the two that did surface a couple years ago, most of the evidence had been washed away by the salty water of the St. John's River.

Haley Tidwell simply vanished. No blood, no evidence of any kind really, at least none that suggested a crime had been committed. She recalled the scuff marks on the bed frame, though, how Abraham had somehow known she'd seen something, and now it was gone. Everything in that room was gone, conveniently. And then there was the acetone, the bleach, she knew he had used them to make chloroform, but again could not prove it. No chloroform had been found in the house either, but she hoped, prayed, that if his car was found, some form of trace evidence might be found inside. There were a lot of doubts surrounding that as well. He was smarter than that.

Then, of course, there was the trust fund, now closed out. Why? Because he was running, she knew, and now he had the money to go anywhere he wanted. He could change his name, his looks, disappear without a trace, until another body showed up, or another girl went missing. That, she was sure, would happen. Men like Abraham could not stop. Something lived inside them that she had never been able to understand, thankfully.

Then there were the tragedies on the Fourth of July.

His father, Henry Kinsinger, had deserted Abraham and his mother on the Fourth.

Then, his mother, Helena, had died in an *accidental* fire on the Fourth. Mahan wondered if that fire had indeed been an accident, doubted it actually, but again, had no proof. Never would, without a confession.

But what about the couple in the parking lot of the Ramada the night of the Fourth? Could they positively identify Abraham as being the man they saw in the parking lot, dragging the suitcase, *with Haley Tidwell crammed inside?*

And Joanie Hernandez, the receptionist at the hotel, would she be able to identify him as being the man that confronted her at the counter, just before the surveillance tapes went missing?

Probably, she said aloud.

But they had to find Abraham Kinsinger first.

She called EP again, and suggested using the

media again. They had other pictures of Abraham, more recent, and in far better quality than the sketch or the blurred image from the security cameras at the Ramada. They also had his name, and she wanted to use the media to alert the public to contact them if they've seen him. He agreed, but wanted to call his father first. Not for permission, but just so Stephen Kidder would not be caught off guard. It was, she knew, their only chance, their only hope at finding the man she deemed a *maniac*. He was a monster, she knew, and needed to be *putdown*.

EP gave her the number to his contact at the *St. Augustine Record*, a woman, Miranda Richardson. Her attitude was flashy, and she was eager to propel her career to a bigger publisher.

A story like this would help, Mahan thought. *Miranda Richardson will do anything I want.*

*

"If I knew where he was, I'd tell you detective Kidder." Miguel lied. "It's not like him not to show up for work...."

"He's probably not coming back. Abraham had a trust fund, it's cleaned out." EP saw Miguel's eyes twitch and his hands resumed trembling. "You better start taking me seriously, and for your safety, I suggest you contact us if he does try and get in contact with you." He edged closer, looked Miguel right in the eyes and pointed a finger in his face. "You're life could be in danger. Believe it or not, Abraham Kinsinger is dangerous."

"I don't believe it."

Disgusted, Kidder turned and walked away. He called the office, asked for a team of deputies to drop by Miguel Hampton's house and check the place out. He doubted Abraham would hide out there, he'd be stupid to.

And he did not think Abraham was stupid.

Still, he had to be sure.

---

*

Franklin Tidwell did not wake up until four o'clock in the afternoon, and not on his own accord either.

His drinking was out of control.

His wife was in the room, disgusted at the sight of him, and they had not spoken a word to each other in days. She shook him again, told him to get his ass up, and explained Detective Kantz was on his way over with news.

"Have they found Haley?" His head throbbed but he climbed out of bed and wobbled to the bathroom, started pissing with the bathroom door open, neglecting to lift the seat. He asked the question without care, his tone ice-cold, and without worry. Molly did not know if he was asking out of concern, wondering if she was indeed found, dead or alive? But when he continued, he left no doubt. "Cause if not, I wish that fat asshole would just leave us alone."

She did not want to, but Molly ignored his tone. "He wouldn't discuss it over the phone, but apparently, they've made progress in the investigation."

"And?"

"It didn't sound good Frank...."

Frank checked his cell phone to see if *Angelo* had called. No one had, and that disappointed him. He sat on the edge of the bed and surveyed his wife. "I'm fucking hungry. Think he'll bring us a pizza."

"Our daughter could be dead and you're

worried about eating a pizza? Why don't you order some more chicken wings and have them delivered to the room?"

"Huh?" He didn't know what she was talking about.

"The other night, while you were at the hotel bar, you ordered some fucking chicken wings to the room. Your drunken ass wasn't even here. You're out of control Frank, and it's got to stop. You are going downhill. Our daughter is missing, maybe dead, and you did things to her that I can't even imagine. Like it or not, it's destroying you inside. You have to do something about it."

"Fuck you Molly." Frank could care less about what he had done to his daughter. That was in the past. He wondered though, *did I really order those fucking chicken wings?* Then he checked his phone again, just to make sure no one had called. Molly could have gone through his phone while he was sleeping. He would not put it past the bitch. It appeared she had not though, and then instead of worrying over Haley, he pondered, *is Angelo pulling my leg?*

Molly could tell Frank's mind was elsewhere.

"You need to be punished for what you did Frank. Maybe I should tell Detective Kantz what you told me when he gets here...."

That got Frank's attention.

He jumped from the bed, grabbed Molly by the throat and pushed her against the wall. "If you do," he warned convincingly. A dabble of spit had accumulated at the corner of his mouth. "I will find a way to kill you."

After that, Molly began to sob, and he let go.

He went back to the bathroom and climbed in the shower. He whistled a tune, Molly could hear it from the room, *Andy Griffith*, she thought. She turned on the television to try and drown out the noise.

He better not be pulling my leg, Frank hissed, the argument with his wife already forgotten, he knew she would not say anything. *Angelo better come through with some pussy!*

*

The restaurant Fiddler's Green was a tad more crowded than the time Mahan and EP had visited, but she still had no trouble finding Miranda Richardson at the bar, sipping on a apple martini. She had fiery red hair, wavy, and lengthy past her shoulders. Her complexion was pale, and light freckles spackled rosy cheeks, bringing out her distinctive, cat-like, greenish-yellow eyes. She wore a short blue dress, that was hemmed just before her knees, and cleavage sparkled with a hint of glitter in the dimly lit bar. She was the most attractive woman in the room, and she worked the bar well.

"Mahan? Over here," Miranda called and ordered another drink. Mahan's badge and gun had given her away. "It's nice to meet you." They exchanged pleasantries and then the redhead went to work. "So, EP gave you my number huh? Must be important. You say you need my help?" She knew a story was on the brink, could feel it, and whipped out her notepad and a pen. "Is this going to be on the record?"

"It will be…."

"I'm afraid I don't understand?"

"I can't give you the *full* story right now. I'm sorry, but the investigation isn't complete, and it just wouldn't be ethical for me to give you all the details right now. There could be other lives at stake."

Miranda looked skeptical, disappointed, and a little angry. Mahan continued. "But I promise you, if you work with me, when all this is over, I'll give you everything, all of it…."

"I'm listening agent Pierce…"

"I need you to run a story, get it on the air and in the papers. I got a name, and a picture of a guy who is a person of interest in our investigation. We need to find this guy, it's important, and we want the public to be our eyes and ears. They can help us find him. *You* can help us find him." She handed over a picture of Abraham Kinsinger.

"Good looking guy," Miranda admitted. "Ok, I'm in. How exactly do you want *this* piece to go?" Mahan told her exactly what she wanted, promised it would be worth her while in the end. "Why exactly are you trying to find Abraham Kinsinger?"

"Off the record?"

"For now, yes."

"We have reason to believe he's a serial killer." Mahan watched as Miranda's eyebrows rose. She did not know it, but she licked her lips. "We got a total of six missing women that we know of…."

"Any bodies?"

"Off the record, yes, two. Found a few years ago."

"And you've made a connection with Kinsinger?"

"Yes, but it's not a strong one, yet. But I'm telling you, this is the kind of story that can make a career. Just be patient with the details for now, I will give you the story of a lifetime when we get this guy."

"By *we*, do you mean you and Detective Kidder?"

"Yes, he's involved." Mahan sipped the apple martini. She liked it. "Is that important?"

"No, but it helps."

Mahan was curious. "Why is that?"

"Because he's got a tight little ass and gorgeous ocean-like blue eyes," Miranda did not mind speaking her mind. She was entitled to fantasize. She continued, nonchalantly, completely catching Mahan off guard. "So tell me. Have you fucked him yet?"

"No," Mahan did not know why she answered the question, but did. *I've thought about it.* "Have you?"

Miranda laughed, but did not answer.

Bitch, Mahan thought. *Redheaded bitch!*

16

Kidder could have slept until noon, would have, if his phone hadn't jolted the still air. He saw it was Jimmy Kantz and grunted. His eyes were heavy, and they wanted to close again. "What is it?"

"Think we found the car..."

"You think?"

"Can't be sure just yet, but it's got to be it. Abandoned at a camping sight next to a marsh off the 206 near Crescent Beach. He torched it, burned to a fucking crisp."

"Do I need to be there?"

"Yes Kidder, you should."

"Why?"

"Because I think there are two bodies in it."

*

Abraham wished he would have done things a little differently.

He figured he had a day, maybe two at the most before the FBI *cunt* and Kidder found his car. It may take them a while to identify it as his, but they eventually would, he knew, and they would also find the bodies....*in my goddamn car!*

He had fucked up, he knew now.

I should have taken the bodies with me, disposed of them somewhere else, somewhere where they'd never be found or traced to me.

It was too late for that. They were in his car, and they would know he killed them.

Now it was official, there was no turning back.

But he had known this day would eventually come, even expected it, just not so soon.

The bodies were indeed a mistake though. Before the slip up, he was certain all the *piggies* had on him were rifled speculations and circumstantial coincidences at best. Until now, they had no bodies, except the two he'd purposely discarded in the St. John's River, and he felt comfortable the others would never be found. He had even buried his Colt .45 in the backyard before he fled, and destroyed every piece of clothing or furniture that might have any trace evidence on them. Until now, nothing had been left behind, nothing concrete anyway. He had been nearly perfect.

Nearly perfect…..

His world was crumbing, as it had to all the *others.*

But the Ruger .9mm would do, if he ever needed to use it, it was a decent gun. But he hoped he never had to pull the trigger.

Killing people with guns was too easy.

Joyless.

Unless he had to take himself out.

And he would, if he had to, if backed into a corner. He would never wind up like the *others.*

*

Mahan had agreed to meet EP and Tuesday at the campsite where the car had been found, but something else caught her attention. She passed a Blockbuster, turned around and pulled into the parking lot. She had a hunch, but kept her fingers crossed as she walked inside.

It was early afternoon, business was slow.

She asked for a manager, but there was not one

on duty at the moment. "Not here," Sara, the clerk replied. Her hair was black, with two purple stripes flowing down the center. Purple eye shadow hid her light-green eyes, and black lipstick smeared the oval mouth ring in her bottom lip. "Just little old me." She noticed the gun and badge. "FBI?" Mahan nodded. "Wow. Thought you guys only existed in the movies." Spunky, and *punky*, Mahan thought. "Is something wrong? I can try to reach my manager over the phone if you need to speak with him."

"Maybe you can help me?"

"Me? How?"

"Can your system do a search for movie titles and cross reference customers who have checked them out? It's important."

"I might be able to figure that out, I guess….you sure I don't need to call my boss first?"

"Feel free, I got all day. But it's just a favor. You'd be helping me out. You could be a major contributor to this investigation." The reluctance settled and the girl agreed to help. Mahan told her what she needed. "I need to know the names of any clients that have rented any titles pertaining to serial killers. Any and all of them. I need to know if the same man rented these films."

"I got a better way," Sara snickered and touched her tongue to her lip ring. "That's too confusing, if you don't mind my saying so."

Mahan didn't. "Go on."

"Why don't you give me a name, if you have one, and I'll see if he's in our database? If so, I can give you a printout of his entire rental history."

"Now why didn't I think of that?" Mahan asked and Sara answered by shrugging her shoulders. Then put her hands on the keyboard waiting for the name to follow. "Abraham Kinsinger." Mahan crossed her fingers again but felt a positive aura flowing around her. She would have to come back with a court order, she knew, to make it official….legal.

"Yep, he's in here. Hold on, this'll just take a sec."

*

"Kidder, watch your step. You should've worn boots."

And he should have. There was a lot of ash, he could still smell the remnants of blistered metal, and his nostrils fielded smoke and an unmistakable hint of burned flesh. It had also started to drizzle slightly, and the ground was damp. His deck shoes bore no traction. "M.E. hasn't arrived yet?"

"You're the first," Kantz answered, still gazing into the car. He did notice Mahan was not with him, thought that was odd and wondered where she was. "You run her off already?"

"She's on her way big man." EP had reached the car and peered inside, careful not to touch anything, or elaborate on his growing relationship with Mahan. He saw what he knew were two skulls, no flesh remained, but they were skulls nonetheless. Kantz had been right about the bodies, and the shape of the scorched automobile did resemble a Buick LeSabre, but they would need further testing to be sure. "Crime scene on the way?"

"Yeah, I called them before I called you. Is everybody dragging ass today? I thought that was a trait reserved for me and my faulty liver."

"Call them back, this is priority." EP paused and looked out over the marsh. "Poor bastards. It's peaceful out here. I bet these two were just camping, enjoying nature or each other last night when Kinsinger surprised them. I bet they never had a chance."

"He did need to ditch his car though because we were going to find him. Smart."

"Not really. If this is his car, he's left us two bodies. That's not like him, he's normally more careful than this. We got him running, and it cost these two people their lives."

"It's not our fault Kidder. But even if we can't hang him on the other missing girls, we'll bury his ass with these two bodies. There's no way out now."

"Okay," EP started replaying the scene as Mahan arrived. He noticed something in her hand. "Let's assume this is Kinsinger's car. We got two bodies, torched, surely to destroy evidence. Assuming these two were camping, we must assume he killed them, and then set them ablaze inside his car. There might be some blood around here somewhere, don't let anyone else down here okay Jimmy?" Kantz nodded. "And they had to be driving something, so let's assume Kinsinger stole it, and move on that. We need to find out who they are and what they were driving. Let's check missing person reports, and keep checking them until someone reports something. We have two bodies, two people missing. Someone will come looking for them sooner or later."

*

Stephen Kidder was boisterously dramatic, but not for affect, he simply wanted to be heard. "Two more bodies Ernest? You want to tell me what the fuck is going on. I'm going out on a limb for you, but if you can't handle it, by God I'll find someone who can." He wasn't finished, just needed a moment, his heart fluttered violently, and a sudden dizziness brought him to his chair in his office. "And this Miranda Richardson bitch is going to burn us. People will listen to whatever it is she has to say, whatever she writes. Have you seen the rack on that woman?"

"This is Mahan's call, and I'm backing her on it dad." EP stood firm, but wished the phone call would end. He had already dismissed the idea of Sunday dinner the coming weekend. Wasn't worth it, and he did not want to hear it. "We'll dictate the story she writes."

"Fucking reporters. You can't trust them, and you know that!"

"I also know that this asshole is going to keep killing until we stop him, and we need all the help we can get. He's not waiting until the next Fourth of July anymore, *we* messed that up dad. And we have to use any means necessary to bring him down. But we'll get him. We're getting closer everyday."

"I got a question for you son," Stephen was still livid, and his tone told EP the conversation was about to end. He said nothing, just waited for the ridicule. "Who's going to die tomorrow?"

The line went dead.

EP answered anyway.

Hopefully Abraham Kinsinger.

He did not want to ruin his handcuffs.

*

Mahan heard everything.

"Don't worry about your father. He'll get over it." She handed him the list she had gotten from Blockbuster as they pulled into The Pink Flamingo, the newer restaurant on San Marco Ave. "Unbelievable, this *maniac* has rented *every* title they have on serial killers."

That did not surprise Kidder at all, and he shrugged his shoulders. He was more worried about Miranda Richardson, and what information Mahan had leaked. "So the story is going to air on the five o'clock news? You sure you got her in your palms?"

"Had to promise an exclusive when this shit is over, but yeah, Miranda will be all right. You know her don't you? I got the sense the two of you have a history?" She was prying now, not realizing it.

"Yeah I know her."

"That it?"

"What else would there be? Our jobs have intersected a time or two over the years." EP saw the skepticism in Mahan's eyes, but it was the chewing of her bottom lip that surprised him as they sat at the table and ordered drinks. He had never seen that from Mahan before, a sign of weakness....*jealousy?* "You ok Agent Pierce?"

"I will be."

Kidder's phone rang and he held up a finger, smiled. It was Tuesday. "Don't tell me there's another body Jimmy."

"No, but we might as well kill this asshole...."

"I don't get it bud."

"Henry Kinsinger is here, at the station, and I want to put a bullet in him. Far as I'm concerned, let's pin everything on him."

"We're on the way."

As Mahan and EP left, the five o'clock news had just begun, and within seconds, an attractive image of Miranda Richardson filled the screen showing a picture of Abraham Kinsinger, and asking the public to notify the authorities of his whereabouts as he was wanted for questioning in the disappearance of Haley Tidwell. She described him not as a suspect, but as a person of interest, a potential material witness.

And they should not have left.

Had they stayed, they would have heard one of the hostesses speak out. "Oh my God, he was here. That guy, that guy right there on the television. He was here. He bought wings and one of our shirts and a hat. I can't believe it."

"Oh whatever, you watch too many crime shows," a waitress snarled back. She was too busy to keep up, and more people needed to be seated. The *bitch* needed to do her job and stop watching television.

"I swear it was him," the hostess felt stupid, wished she had kept her comments to herself, and wanted the waitress to slip and fall…..wanted her to feel embarrassed. It was not fun. No one seemed to like her at work.

She kept the rest of her thoughts to herself.

And never called the police.

It was him though, she thought as she sat another couple where the empty chairs from Mahan and EP now sat. *I know it was him.*

*

Kidder sensed Henry Kinsinger was coming down from something. His eyes were bloodshot and his pupils were dilated. His gray hair was a mess and oily, had not been washed in days, maybe even a week. He was a skinny man, carried a weak frame, and patches of gray facial hair dotted his face unevenly. EP was sure a strong wind could knock him off his feet. The sight of Henry saddened him, and he noticed a distinct, musky, onion-like odor as soon as he walked into the interrogation room. He wore a pair of stained blue jeans and a long sleeved red and black checkered shirt, also dirty. He opened his mouth to take a sip of water and EP also noticed a decaying set of rotten teeth. *Maybe Abraham was better off without this scumbag in his life*, he thought. "Thanks for coming Mr. Kinsinger. I hope the drive wasn't all bad, and wish we could have met under better circumstances.

"Just get on with it detective," Henry had finished his water, wanted more, and motioned for Kidder to make it happen by sliding the empty paper cup across the table. "You got my ass down here. Might as well just get on with it."

"It's about your son, Abraham." EP motioned for a uniformed officer to refill the cup of water, he also asked for a diet Coke.

"I ain't got no son Detective."

"Yes you do, of your own flesh and blood. His name is Abraham Kinsinger, almost thirty years old, and abandoned by you twenty-eight years ago." EP paused as the officer put the drinks down in front of them and then leaned across the table to connect with the homeless looking man in front of him. "Guys like you disgust me. You just walk out on your wife and kid and never look back. He was your child Henry. Your son. You didn't want to watch him grow into a man? Never wanted to teach him to ride a bike, or play catch?"

"Listen, you weren't there." Henry was going to defend himself. "Times were hard, and I got mixed up in shit that I let get out of control. Abraham and Helena, both of them, were better off without me."

"I think you're a coward." EP was honest, and felt certain the *shit* Henry had been mixed up in was drugs. He assumed they still played a prevalent role in his meaningless life. "You had the chance to do something great, something real and exciting. You had the chance to be a father and you turned your back on your family. Unforgivable if you ask me."

"Well I'm not asking you, but thanks for the parenting lecture. You don't know what I've been through. You couldn't possibly understand. But it's easy for you to sit there and pass judgment on someone like me, because I've had a harder life than you. Well, let me ask you something Detective Kidder," Henry paused and laid his palms flat on the table. "You got any children of your own? You ever done anything you regret?"

"This is not about me." EP smiled, sipped his diet Coke. He found it refreshing.

"Well this ain't about me either." Henry's voice was deep, hardened after years of poverty and disappointment. "I thought you brought me down here to ask me questions about Abraham?" Henry was right, EP knew, and forced the tongue lashing to come to an end, or at least pause. It was not his job to pass judgment on Henry Kinsinger. It was his job to find his son, Abraham. "I'll tell you what I know, but it ain't going to be much. I have not seen or spoken with him since he was a boy, not since his mother died."

"Did he seem upset about that....the death of his mother?"

"I really can't recall." EP thought he was genuinely trying to remember. "That whole time period is like a blur. Between you and me, I was hooked on them damn pain killers. They had my whole world fucked up."

I was right, drugs.

"You could've gotten help Henry."

"I know, I know," he put his hands over his face and pulled them down past his chin and then put them back on the table. "But can we please not go back down that road again. I know how you feel about me, you've made it clear, and I can see the hate in your eyes. Believe it or not, I think you're right. I'm a piece of shit. I'm aware of it. A walking, breathing, stank piece of shit. And I wake up hating myself more and more everyday. So just keep the insults to yourself. Not only are they a waste of time, but I'm going to be so fucked up thirty minutes after I leave here that I won't even remember a word you said."

"How about I knock some fuc-" EP was interrupted by the sound of the door opening. Mahan stepped inside seconds later and asked to speak with him in private. He followed her into the hallway. "I keep forgetting this guy isn't a suspect and that he came here to help us. It's hard to keep my cool in there." He finished with a finger pointing towards the door to the interrogation room, and then balled a hardened fist.

"Well, let someone else take a run at him," Mahan replied. "You think he's going to be able to help us find Abraham?"

"Doubt it. But it's worth a try." Then, EP shifted directions. "What did you need me for?"

"Might have a break on the bodies we found in the car at the campsite. A distraught mother just walked through the door wanting to fill out an MPR." Mahan had the *missing person's report* in her hand. "Her name is Lou Ellen McElroy, says her son left the other night with his girlfriend and neither one of them has come home. No phone calls, nothing."

"Man, this isn't going to be good."

"There's more," Mahan squeezed his hand. She saw the sadness in EP's eyes. It was never easy to inform parents they their children were believed to be dead. "She says the two were last seen packing up the girlfriend's car…..They were going camping Ernest. Near Crescent Beach….."

"Ok," EP said and cleared his throat. He went back inside the interrogation room for his diet Coke, and told Henry someone else would be there soon to ask him a few more questions. Henry agreed, but made it clear that he wanted to leave soon. Once back in the hallway, he took the report from Mahan. "Let's get this over with."

"Yes. Let's go find out who they are."

"And what kind of car they were driving."

*

Abraham walked away from the Honda CRV when he saw the taxi pull into the parking lot. He did not know if it was the boy or girl's phone he had used, nor did he care. He planned on leaving it in the cab anyway, tucked under the seat, and powered *on.*

He flailed his arms in the air to get the cab driver's attention.

It worked.

"Car trouble?" the driver said. "Where are we headed today?"

"Not sure yet," Abraham admitted. He was just happy to ditch the car. He was sure they would be looking for him in it by now. "Just drive friend. I'll let you know when we get there."

The driver thought the request was unusual, but pulled out of the parking lot anyway and tapped the meter. "It's your dime friend. Your dime."

"Just drive." He took the safety off the Ruger.

Then, under his breath, he added, *it's your life friend. Your life.*

There is nothing more devastating than realizing your child is never coming home. Whether prepubescent, teenaged, or fully grown, there is something disheartening inside to know your child will never walk through the front door again. Pain, as always, yields in time, but of course when dealing with matters of the heart, they never truly go away. There is always the birthday on the calendar, that is the worst day of all, but every holiday brings just as much pain as it does joy, and of course there are countless movie titles that must be rendered into the world of forgetfulness. No matter what, though, the mind passionately holds on to the memories of loved ones, both good and bad, forever embroidered on the faces of timeless tombstones.

Barry McElroy's mother, Lou Ellen, was in the beginning stages of this grief, and with that came confusion, distrust, anger, sadness, pain, and the refusal to believe something *bad* had happened. However, she knew *something* was wrong, had felt it the morning she woke up and made breakfast for her son. He had promised to be home in time for breakfast, and he was supposed to bring his girlfriend along, Savannah Clayton. Lou Ellen had been looking forward to meeting her, knew her son had been seeing her for a few months, and it seemed serious, or serious enough for a twenty year old, but this was supposed to be the first time they would meet.

But morning slowly drifted into the afternoon, and the breakfast had grown cold, but remained on the counter. Lou Ellen knew it would only take a moment to heat it up in the microwave. She would have discarded the meal all together, actually, and made a couple ham and turkey clubs sandwich's for lunch if they preferred. She was not mad, just wanted her son to come home, wanted them both to be okay. She hated it when he went camping, but he loved it, his father had been taking him since he was four years old, and after Barry's father had passed suddenly from a heart attack, he'd continued camping, it was how he dealt with the loss of his father, she knew, and she never dared trying to convince him to stop.

She had been calling his cell phone, of course, non-stop, and left countless messages.

Nothing.

That's when she knew something was wrong. Barry had always returned her calls, even when he was in trouble, he always called back….always.

Then, as afternoon turned to dusk, she tried calling a couple of his friends. But no one had seen him. Finally, feeling frantic and drenched with the dread of knowing *something* had happened, she tried the police. But they had told her he had not been missing long enough to fill out an MPR. She would not listen, she was a mother, and her instinct told her something was wrong. The officer on the phone explained that it could be something as simple as car trouble, even suggested Barry and his girlfriend could have run away together.

That was not possible, Lou Ellen knew.

Her son would never do that.

"If my son said he went camping officer," she had snapped into the phone. "Then that's what he did! And if he told me that he was going to be home in the morning, then he would have showed up. Unless," her voice dropped and a lump had grown in her throat. It had been hard for her to continue. "Unless something has happened."

Persistence finally paid off, though, and the officer agreed to send a few patrol cars out to known campsites to see if they could find the couple, or spot the silver Honda CRV. "For now," she was told. "That was all they could do."

And now she was at the police station, had been put in a room.

They had found something, she knew, the way the other officers had looked at her when she walked through the door and announced why she was there had said it all. *They'd found something,* she rattled the thought around in her head, and tried to prepare herself for the worst. *They know what happened to my son.*

*

"So you mean to tell me this lady phoned in and reported her son missing a day ago?" Mahan used a nod to answer EP's question. "And dispatch was supposed to send a few patrolmen out to campsites to look for this missing couple?" She nodded again. "Then why the fuck weren't they found a day ago? Fuckin' Kinsinger has had twenty-four extra hours to bend us over...." He wanted to calm down before he entered the room. The whole situation pissed him off, and this time, when answering, Mahan only shrugged her shoulders. "Unbelievable. I want somebody's ass on a platter for this." He sounded like his father, but again did not realize it.

Then, they entered the interview room, and Lou Ellen looked up at them with weathered eyes. *She already knows,* Kidder thought. *She already knows her son is dead.* "Can I get you anything? Water? Soda? Anything at all?"

"I'm ok," she mumbled, and she took a moment to hold a balled fist to her mouth as she cleared her throat. "Do you know something Detective Kidder? Do you know what happened to my son?"

EP told her the truth. He explained he could not be sure until they made a positive ID on the bodies, but did suggest that he believed it to be the bodies of Barry McElroy and Savanna Clayton. She hugged him as he continued, and agreed to help them find articles around her house that could be used for DNA testing.

Mahan immediately volunteered to escort the woman home. She wanted to handle any and all evidence herself. The chain of command would go through her alone, and eventually, she wanted to input any evidence pertaining to Kinsinger, or any victims into CODIS, the FBI's national *Combined DNA Index System*. She knew any biological, mitochondrial, or forensic evidence left behind might help generate enough leads to get ahead of Kinsinger. It was a useful tool, and Mahan was considered an expert.

When the interview was over, Mahan escorted the distraught mother outside, and gave EP an encouraging wink. Lou Ellen had wanted to see the bodies, but he had assured her that nothing good would come from it. The remains of both victims were charred, unrecognizable.

He sighed and looked at his notepad.

He'd written two names.

Barry McElroy and Savannah Clayton.

Both twenty years old.

Both probably dead! Wrong place, wrong time.

He had also written down the make and model of Savannah's car, a silver Honda CRV. Every law enforcement officer in the state and beyond would be searching for it in a matter of minutes.

Then, he looked at the names of Savannah's parents.

Eugene and Ally Clayton.

He did not want to do what came next.

He had to go see the Clayton's......and inform them of the possibility that their daughter was dead.

<u>17</u>

St. George Street never changed. People were everywhere, wasting money on touristy treasures that would sit on display for a while in their homes, atop fireplace mantles collecting dust, only to be discarded of later, or tucked away into a cardboard box and forgotten about. Abraham never understood why people bought useless shit. But then again, he did not care either, the opening of purses and wallets helped him blend in. Still, his picture had been all over the news, he knew, so he kept a red baseball cap pulled low, and wore big framed sunglasses. No one would notice him, they never did.

He had told the cab driver to drop him off at the college, Flagler, a couple blocks from St. George Street, but the walk had been a short one, and uninterrupted for the most part. He had left the cell phone on, under the seat of the cab, and knew the *piggies* would be spending the next few hours trying to track it. That, he knew, would give him enough time. *Perfect.*

He paid for a piece of pizza and casually sat alone at a table.

He pulled the cheese off first and inhaled it with a couple of bites. Then he stared down at his plate and ate what was left. Only the dough and a seasoned red marinara sauce remained. He licked his lips and poked at the dough. The dough reminded him of human flesh, and the sauce vividly resembled blood. He thought about everyone he had killed, closed his eyes in an attempt to relive every detail, and found the entire situation erotic.

The itch came back as he devoured the

pizza…..*the flesh and blood.*

Behind his sunglasses, he watched people walk by. Everyone was smiling and happy. Alive.

He could kill them, he knew, if he really wanted to.

Then he thought about Haley Tidwell.

He thought about her a lot.

Their time together had come to an end too soon.

But their time together had been beautiful. The feel of her porcelain skin, the taste of her perfumed flesh was enough to drive *any* man mad.

He thought about going to her.

Maybe just one more visit, he thought, *before everything is gone? No! It's doing stupid shit like that that got us here in the first place you moron. Do you want to get caught?*

He hated it when he had to curse himself, and in the end, he knew it was far too risky to try and visit her.

Then, he tried to think about what he needed to do next.

Goddamn it, he fumed silently. An erection was halting his efforts to think clearly. He got up, and pulled his shirt down as low as he could to try and hide the bulge in his pants. It would not go away, he knew, until he made it. He found the nearest bathroom and empty stall and stepped inside, locking the door behind him. There were a couple other men in the restroom relieving themselves, but he was undeterred.

He had his cock in his hands seconds later, and let his pants fall all the way to his ankles.

Abraham massaged himself violently, and grunted a few times.

He thought about Haley, wanted to be inside of

her again.

Then, moments later, it was over. His hand was covered by a blanket of warm semen and he shook as much as he could into the toilet, leaving some on the rim. He wiped off as best he could before exiting the stall and flushed. He found someone waiting for the vacancy and nodded as he walked out the door.

He heard the stranger scream "mother fucker," as he sat down on the toilet, now laced with a few sediments of Abraham's semen, but he paid no attention, and casually strolled away.

He still thought about Haley Tidwell, and how she did things to him that none of the *others* had been willing to do, no matter how much he tried to force them. There were certain times where it seemed as though she were actually trying to please him.

And she did.

Abraham couldn't help but wonder if he would ever feel that again ....*wanted?*

Now, however he needed to find a car.

He did not want to leave Franklin Tidwell waiting any longer, and hoped the drunken asshole did not pay attention to the news.

If he had, Abraham knew, he would be the one getting fucked.

*

Kidder returned to the station from the Clayton's house an hour later, and handed the evidence bags over to Mahan. "Does it ever get any easier? I can't imagine what those parents must be feeling. I'm scared to death of having children for this very reason."

"You can't let bad people cloud your judgment

on how wonderful life can be. And although I don't have any children of my own, I've been told that it's the absolute most wonderful feeling in the world. Everyone says that nothing brings them more joy than their children. At least that's what my mother always tells me. Sometimes I think she still thinks I'm seven."

"You'll always be her little girl, no matter how big and fat you get from eating all those crab claws."

"Not funny." Mahan jabbed EP on the shoulder and they both laughed for a second. They needed that, and it did them some good. "But to answer your question," she continued truthfully. "No. It never gets any easier. That's why it's our job to catch these *animals*, so that the families of the victims can have closure. It helps them to know what happened, instead of having to wonder about it. And they also take a form of satisfaction, I think, in knowing that when the person is caught, that they can never harm another person again. It's not until we catch these creeps, that the families began the healing process. After we do our job, they can begin to focus on all the good memories they have, instead of just on what has happened. At least that's what I think."

"Want to know what I think?" Kidder asked, but was going to tell her anyway.

He was interrupted. "You aren't going to believe this shit." Tuesday's voice was loud, and riddled with excitement.

"What is it Jimmy?" EP winked at Mahan, he would finish talking to her later….when they were back at his place.

"So, I'm on my way back over to the Ramada to check in with the Tidwell's when an officer calls my cell phone with news. And there's something going on over there by the way, just throwing that out there, but something definitely is not right with those two," Kantz had changed subjects, referring to Frank and Molly Tidwell. "Every time I go see them, there's a look in Mrs. Tidwell's eyes, like she's asking me for help or something, and Mr. Tidwell is just a sorry asshole. I'm not sensing any emotion from that guy whatsoever. Gives me the creeps, really. Thought about shooting him. Anyway, they are not going to be staying in town much longer, but something is definitely going on there and I want that on the record. I don't know if he's beating her, or what's happened in their past, but that dirt bag is definitely hiding something." Kantz stated, rather than questioned as his rant concluded.

"Did we ever get anything from Haley's psychiatrist?"

"Nope," Tuesday was running out of breath. "Won't give us much. But the good old doctor will tell us that the majority of their sessions have been spent merely getting to know one another. She said that she and Haley hadn't reached the pinnacle moment of opening up yet, and also implied that even if they had, I wouldn't be able to get anything from her anyway without a court order. And even then, probably nothing."

"We can force our way into her records if we have too," Mahan was certain. Her employers were powerful, definitely persuasive.

EP jumped back to the matter at hand. "Back to what you were saying when you walked in here Jimmy. What kind of shit am I not going to believe?"

"Oh yeah, sorry. We found the car," Kantz smiled. "We found Savannah Clayton's silver Honda CRV."

"Well let's go." Kidder motioned for Tuesday to ride with him, he knew Mahan wanted to stay behind and process the evidence. "I'll drive. I'll even buy you a cup of coffee partner."

"Well in that case, just walk your happy ass over to the coffee machine and pour me a cup because we ain't got to drive anywhere." Kantz stood matter-of-factly and crossed his arms. He was serious about the coffee though. "I like lots of cream and sugar, and don't you dare hold out on me. LOT'S OF CREAM AND SUGAR Kidder!"

"Am I missing something?"

"The car is in the fucking parking lot outside!" Kantz blurted, prepared to make his own cup of coffee, figured Kidder would just screw it up anyway. "Sonofabitch drove it right to us!"

"Well isn't that precious. Remind me to send this guy a thank you note." EP was pissed. Kinsinger was making this personal, he knew, was bringing the fight to them, showing them that he was not afraid.

"This guy is going to bust our balls isn't he?" Tuesday asked.

"Mine are *blue* already!"

Once on the elevator, Tuesday nudged EP's elbow and questioned. "So, about your nuts? Are they *blue* from Kinsinger or agent Pierce? She's got a stellar rack if you ask me. You are one fortunate cocksucker."

"Do you really want to see my balls Jimmy?" EP could dish it out just as fast as Tuesday could throw it. "Seriously? They're nice. You wanna see them?"

"Fucking asshole!"

18

"Hey, you guys get anything in the car?" Mahan asked in a hurried voice over the cell phone.

"Forensic team is going through it now, bout to haul it to the lab. So far nothing out of the ordinary. We got some fingerprints, but no signs of blood."

"Well stay there, I'm on my way down!" Mahan ordered rather than asked EP. He did not take it that way. "I think we may have something. Got a trace on a cell phone belonging to one of our victims, Barry McElroy. It's on, we can track it."

"Are you serious?" Kidder could not believe it, sounded too easy.

"I'm as serious as a heart attack. And it's close by, near campus!"

*

"I didn't think you were actually going to call me." Franklin Tidwell did not recognize the number, figured it had to be *Angelo Richards*. It was. "My wife and I are going to be leaving town soon, I was hoping you were going to come through. What number are you calling me from anyway?"

"A pay phone," Abraham admitted. He liked being *Angelo Richards*. "Does it really matter?"

"No, no. Of course not. Are we going to meet up?"

"Do you have the money?"

"Yes. Do you have the girls?"

"Of course I do, I told you I would Frankie," Abraham was trying to unnerve Franklin Tidwell, though it did not appear to be working. He hated it when anyone other than Miguel Hampton called him *Abe,* and assumed the same must have been true for Frank. It was not. He continued. "I am going to need you to come pick me up though. Think your wife will *let* you use the car?" Abraham hoped bringing the wife into it would work.

It paid off. "I don't have to ask that bitch nothing!" Frank spoke emphatically. He was ready to get laid....even snort a few lines....if that's what it took. "So, where are you *Angelina?*"

"Don't call me that," Abraham hissed angrily. Sure, Angelo was not his real name, but he hated nicknames. He had told Frank his name was Angelo, and that is exactly what he expected to be called. "My name is Angelo, not Ange-fuckin-lina! You got it?"

"Chill friend," Frank laughed sarcastically. "You called me Frankie," he reminded Abraham, and Abraham could tell that Franklin Tidwell was not afraid of him, perhaps even thought he was better than him. "I won't do it again I promise. Just tell me where you're at and I'll come get you."

"I'll be at the Old Fort, across from St. George Street. It's right down the street from you. Just tell me what you're driving, park in the public parking lot right outside the Fort and I'll come to you."

"I know where that is, just watched fireworks from there the night my daughter...." Frank's voice trailed into silence as he thought of his daughter. Abraham could not tell what emotions were going through his head. He wanted to know, badly, and would have been able to if given the chance to look into his eyes.

"Something wrong Frank?"

"No, no. I'll be there in half an hour. Give me a minute to take a shower and change clothes okay? And I'll be driving a red Ford Expedition."

"Take your time friend. And bring some cologne. I could probably use a squirt or two."

"I'm glad you called Angelo," Frank's mood was solemn again. For the first time in days, he was happy, had something to smile about……..albeit another woman's vagina. "Tell me, how old are these girls?"

"Twenty-three, and twenty-five." Abraham tried to remember Haley's age. He was sure she was twenty-three.

"That's perfect. Tonight is going to be the best night of my life."

Franklin Tidwell hung up and Abraham began walking towards the crowd at the Old Fort. He saw a few unmarked police cruisers speed by, sirens and lights alive, clearing all other motorists out of their way. They disappeared around a corner and he continued on his path towards the Fort. He kept replaying Frank's last words in his mind.

Tonight is going to be the best night of my life!

Franklin Tidwell had sounded so positive, so sure….so full of life.

Then, he started singing to himself. It was a tune he recognized, from the holidays when he was a child. He changed the words, of course, to something that suited him a little better.

And he continued to chime away as he waited for Franklin Tidwell to come to him.

Inside his head, each verse grew louder and louder, as the seconds slowly ticked by.

*Over the river and through the wood, to Franklin's soul I go. I know the way to cut out his throat and then leave so no one will know, Oh!….****Over the river and through the wood, to Franklin's soul I go. I know the way to cut out his throat***

and then leave so no one will know,
Oh!....Over the river.........

*

Adam Lundgren welcomed another man into his cab after about an hour of waiting outside the Casa Monica Hotel across the street from Flagler College. It normally did not take that long. The hotel was one of the oldest, and most prestigious in St. Augustine, and the cab driving community considered it a good spot to find business. "Where to friend?" Adam asked as he peered at the man through the rearview mirror. The man before had given him the creeps, there had been something in his eyes, something dark, evil. But this guy seemed different, dark suit and tie, business like, normal.

"Need to get to the amphitheater. Giving a lecture on the history of the Spanish settlers of the area." The man wore stylish, sporty black sunglasses, Costa Del Mar's. Adam had always wanted a pair, but they were two expensive, and groceries seemed more important, to his stomach anyway.

"You got it." Adam pulled away from the curb. "Nice sunglasses," he added as he approached the intersection of San Marco and the newly constructed Bridge of Lions. The light took a couple of minutes, but he turned left just in time to witness three unmarked police cars wail past him and turn in the direction from where he had just had his cab parked.

The man in the backseat smiled. "It's my third pair. Can't seem to take care of the expensive brands, I've lost the other two. But give me a cheap pair from Wal-Mart and for some reason I'll keep them forever.

That ever happened to you?"

"Can't say that it has," Adam admitted as another patrol car sped by. "I've only owned one pair of sunglasses, from Wal-Mart actually."

"See, you'll never need another pair. Good for you."

Then, Adam paused to look into the rearview mirror once again, and saw two of the cars that had just passed heading towards his cab. "What the hell is going on around here today?" He was able to get the question out just as a bevy of red and blue flashing lights flooded his back window. He slowed the cab and pulled towards the curb, expecting the police vehicles to speed by him.

They did not, however, and pursued him to the shoulder, one car parked directly behind him, and the other weaved in front. A voice came over a PA system demanding Adam to turn off the engine and place his hands on the steering wheel. He complied and looked at the man in the backseat. "I don't know what you're into buddy, but next time, take another cab…"

*

"There's someone in the backseat of the cab," EP muttered quickly as he opened the driver side door and stepped out. His revolver was in his hand as he approached the cab from the rear. Mahan was to his right, her gun held at an angle towards the ground, but ready nonetheless in case things turned sour. "I'll take the driver, you take the occupant." She answered with a nod, never taking her eyes off the target.

Five minutes later, it was all over.

Adam had been subdued by EP, thrown to the ground face first, arms handcuffed behind his back.

Mahan had the passenger on the sidewalk second's later, same force applied. "You people are going to hear from my attorney," the man from the backseat of the cab declared emphatically. "And someone is going to be paying for another Armani suit. I demand to know what's going on here."

"It's not Kinsinger," EP scowled, then sat the two men on the curb and removed the handcuffs. He needed to explain what was going on. Tuesday had arrived and started searching the cab. In less than a minute, he found Barry McElroy's cell phone underneath the backseat of the cab. There had not been a major attempt to hide it. EP dialed the number of the cell phone to make sure, and watched as it began vibrating in Tuesday's hand. "We need to get our people on that phone right away Kantz. We need to know what phone calls were made, to who, when, and what was said." Kantz nodded and prepared to leave the scene with the phone and EP turned to face the cab driver and the disgruntled customer. "Was this phone in your possession?" he asked the man from the backseat, where the phone had been found.

"No, that's not my phone," the man answered angrily, and spat a few drops of blood on the ground. His lip was bleeding. "My phone is in my pocket. I demand that you let me go," he hissed and climbed to his feet. "And I need to know your names, identification numbers, and the name and numbers of your superiors for my attorney. We're gong to have a field day with this." The man didn't seem to care that they were looking for a killer…a missing girl.

"What about you?" EP ignored the angry civilian and approached the cab driver. Adam had been silent the whole time, the entire situation had caught him off guard, frightened him. "Did you know this phone was in your cab?"

"No sir, no idea." Adam was honest, his eyes were wide and his mouth had grown dry. "And I clean my cab out every night after my shift. That was not in there yesterday, I'm certain."

"How many people have been in your cab today?"

"Not many, four or five." Adam remembered the man he had just dropped off at the college campus, remembered feeling frightened by him.

"Did any of them look like this?" Mahan handed Adam a picture of Abraham Kinsinger.

"Yes, yes!" Adam exclaimed. *I knew something was wrong with that guy.* "He was the last person in my cab before I picked this guy up. I just dropped him off a little more than an hour ago I think."

"Where?"

Adam pointed towards Flagler College. "At the college or close to it. But I think he was walking towards St. George Street. Weird guy. He freaked me out. I was glad to drop him off. I picked him up from the parking lot of the Sheriff's Department."

"This asshole is enjoying toying with us," EP was furious. He knew Kinsinger had deliberately parked Savannah Clayton's silver Honda CRV in the parking lot of his headquarters, then used Barry McElroy's phone to call a cab, and then left it turned on and placed under the seat of the cab so that they would waste a lot of meaningless time chasing a ghost.

Mahan sensed the tension and let EP walk away for a moment. She overheard him order an officer to give the other man a ride and apologized for the intrusion and forceful tactics. He gave the man a contact number for his attorney, in the event he did want to pursue litigation.

He probably would, she knew, and would probably win. Easy money.

"Do you remember what this man was wearing?" She watched as Adam Lundgren closed his eyes to think. She saw veins sprout along the sides of his temples. "Anything at all Mr. Lundgren. Any detail you can remember is important."

"I don't know why I'm having a hard time with this, he was literally just in my cab."

"It's ok." Mahan warmly gave his shoulder and affectionate squeeze. "Take your time. You didn't pay that much attention to his clothing because you didn't think it was important, that's normal. You didn't know who was in your cab. But your subconscious noticed it, I'm sure. So just take it easy and try to relax. Take a deep breath and start from the beginning, go back to when you first picked him up from the parking lot at the station."

Adam Lundgren came through a few seconds later. "Jeans, I'm sure, a light pair. And I think a collard shirt....black." Mahan nodded, and employed more encouragement as she took notes. "He was also wearing a hat......red one, baseball cap....I think." Adam knew he was right, but the whole situation made him nervous. "And I'm sure he was wearing sunglasses too. I remember that because they were way too big for his face. He took them off in the cab though, and I saw his eyes. After this, I don't think I'm ever going to be able to forget them."

"And you say you think he was heading towards St. George Street?" Mahan asked as a crew arrived to take the cab into their possession. Adam nodded and pointed directly across the street. They were close to the *Old Fort*, and the shopping district was right across the street. "Okay, I'll find you a ride." She frowned as she asked for his keys. "Your cab is going to have to come with us for a little while."

"I want every available officer to report to St. George Street and the campus!" EP took control and began walking across the street, determination looming in his eyes. "I want to sweep this entire area. Put out an APB on the suspect, and what he's wearing. Every store, restroom, classroom, alleyway, and fucking maintenance closet needs to be searched." He phoned dispatch to organize a search. "Let's go get this guy!" Mahan was on his heels as his phone rang again. It was his father, Stephen Kidder. "Now's not a good time."

"You want to tell me what the hell is going on?" His father's tone showed signs of agitation. "I'm getting phone calls from everyone asking why the historical district is being overrun with police cruisers. I got reports from people saying a couple of innocent civilians were being thrown to the ground by a couple of homicidal cops. Are they referring to you son?"

"Yes, we didn't know the situation at first, and proceeded with caution. We had reason to believe that Abraham Kinsinger was within our grasp."

"Was he?"

"A phone belonging to one of the suspected victims was found inside the car, yes. We are certain he was in there, missed him by a few minutes."

"Good job son," the sarcasm stung EP's ears. He thought about hanging up on his father. "Well let me tell you what I know. I know that one of the people you decided to harass is a respected college professor from Florida State University in Tallahassee. His name is Dr. Joseph Andrews, and his attorney is extremely pissed off. We don't need these kinds of headlines son, especially in an election year."

EP held his hand over the phone and spoke to

Mahan. "Cocksucker you slung to the ground has already called his damn attorney. Unbelievable." He knew his father was only worried about their last name, and that troubled him.

"What an asshole."

"Are you hearing me son?" The volume in Stephen's tone had increased twofold. "You're blowing this son. This is your opportunity to make a name for yourself and you are blowing it. Do you have anything to say for yourself?"

"Yes," EP answered calmly, and prepared to end the conversation. "Tell Dr. Andrews to blow me!"

*

Abraham watched the scene unfold from the *Old* Fort, directly across the street, and marveled at how fast the authorities had moved in. He had underestimated Kidder and Mahan's resolve, he knew, but respected them for their diligent pursuit. He was also alarmed at the power of the resources they had at their disposal.

Wasn't fair.

He had watched as EP took down the cab driver, had grown excited as he saw the FBI *bitch* hurl the unbeknownst man in the backseat to the pavement. *Beautiful,* he thought. *They'll never have the chance to do that to me.*

Then, just as he saw a swarm of police officers gather at the North entrance to St George Street, he saw Franklin Tidwell slowly pull his red Ford Expedition into a parking spot in the public lot beside the *Old Fort*. Abraham knew the cab driver must have given the *piggies* a description of his clothing, so he wasted little time. He removed himself from behind a large oak tree, and sprinted towards the

Expedition, using other cars in the parking lot for camouflage.

He was in the passenger seat seconds later, perspiring slightly. *Stupid Florida humidity.*

"What the hell is going on down here?" Franklin Tidwell asked as he noticed the commotion of the police officers across the street.

"Don't know," Abraham lied. "But whatever it is, it seems serious. Think a cab driver is selling drugs or something...."

"Cab driver?" Frank questioned and raised an eyebrow. He handed Abraham his cologne, Polo Sport. He had not forgotten. "If it's concerning a cab driver, could be a damn terrorist...."

"Now don't go stereotyping cab drivers Frankie."

"Yeah yeah." Frank thought about using *Angelina*, but changed his mind. He knew that had pissed him off earlier, and did not want anything to come between him and a good time. "Okay then Angelo Richards. Please tell me where I'm supposed to go."

"Do you have the cash? Probably going to need a couple hundred."

"I don't have that much on me." Frank started the engine, but glared into the eyes of Abraham Kinsinger and continued boldly. "You better not be trying to shake me down Richards. If you are, I promise you will regret it. I am not a man you want to mess with."

Neither am I! I'm going to kill your sorry ass. I'm going to gouge out your eyeballs and cram them down your throat. I'm going to cut your fucking throat and watch you bleed to death, watch every spasm as you choke on your own blood. And then, maybe, just maybe, just to do it, I'm going to rape you, violate you in *ways that you can't even imagine…..just like I did to your precious little girl! But you would know, wouldn't you? Because you've violated her too haven't you? Haven't you, you sick mother fu**…."*

"Do you understand?" Frank sensed *Angelo* was thinking about something, could see it in his eyes, but he did not back down. "You can get out right now and we can forget this whole thing if you don't agree."

"You got nothing to worry about Frank." Abraham found biting his tongue hard, especially in this situation. "I'm not up to anything. Just want to get laid, that's all."

Frank then drove the Expedition out of the parking lot and turned right onto San Marco Avenue, away from the commotion. "Where's the nearest ATM?"

"Just up ahead you'll hang a left, and then turn right onto Ponce de Leon. There are a lot of banks on that road, they all have ATM's."

"Then where?"

"Heaven!" *Angelo Richards* answered plainly, lying through his teeth.

Faking emotions was easy, came naturally.
He answered again, this time to himself.
Hell!

*

Depression, anger, and sadness cemented themselves on Molly Tidwell's shoulders, and it felt like a ton of bricks immobilized her. Confined to the bed, she had not left the hotel room since her daughter had gone missing. She had grown stir crazy, and kept hearing her daughter's voice calling out to her inside her head, though knew in her heart the impossibility of such a phenomenon.

She flipped through all the channels of the television three times, never realizing she had started from the beginning each time.

Her mind was on her daughter; her heart was with Haley, wherever she was, whatever she was doing.

Was she still alive?

No matter what, she could not give up. She would not allow herself to lose hope until someone brought her proof that her daughter was dead. Every once in a while, there was a happy ending. She was a fan of mystery novels, and knew that in the end, there were always a few fortunate survivors.

This could be the same, right?

Then she thought about her husband, Franklin, and how he had grown into a monster over the past few weeks. He had been a monster all along, she knew, although she just realized this a couple of days ago, after he had gotten himself drunk, again, and told her everything. Everything, like how he'd sexually abused their daughter, repeatedly, for years. How he had tiptoed into her bedroom, after he made certain she was sound asleep in their bed, completely oblivious to what was going on down the hall.

I wonder what was going through my baby's mind, she wondered as she pulled the covers to her chin and let a tear fall from her eyes and dampen the pillowcase. *I wonder what Haley was thinking when she saw her father, the man she was supposed to be able to trust above all others, come into the room.*

And why had she never said anything?
Was she scared of him?
Afraid I wouldn't believe her?
Scared of tearing the family apart?

And now, she knew, it was too late. She had to face the very real possibility that she may never know the answers to her questions, had to accept that the sound of her daughter's voice inside her head would haunt her forever.

She also had to accept that her husband, Franklin Tidwell, would get away with it.

No one would ever know what he did.

Unless, she thought. *Unless I do something about it.*

She rolled over in bed and picked up the phone from the nightstand. Detective Jimmy Kantz's card laid next to the phone. She hesitated at first, but grew angrier as the thought of her husband lingered inside her mind. Their daughter was missing, and his decision to go out with a friend he had met in the hotel bar fueled her anger. What was his name, Angelo? Angelo Richards? Well, he had to pay for what he has done. He had to answer for hurting their daughter. She could not remain silent anymore.

Molly Tidwell had to do the right thing. In the end, it was the only thing to do.

The guilt would consume her, maybe even kill her, if she kept the secret any longer.

She dialed the number, already forgiving herself for what she was about to do. "Detective Kantz," she cried into the phone as tears continued to slide down her ashen face. "I'm sorry to bother you. But," she paused to sit up, sniffle, and collect her thoughts. *Do I really want to go through with this?* "I need to talk to you. It's important. It's about my husband, Franklin…."

"Is everything all right?"

"No. I need to talk to you. Please hurry. He confessed everything to me. He hurt my daughter. He did terrible things to her….."

19

Three hours went by.........nothing.

Abraham Kinsinger could have been anywhere. The one place he was not, Kidder was sure, was St. George Street.

"He couldn't have gotten far. I know we're close, we've got to be."

"He wanted us to think he was here," Mahan joined the conversation tired, winded. Her body still felt beaten. "He's been dictating the situation all along. And I'm worried because something just doesn't feel right about this. We're missing something. He's got money, cash, and the means to disappear. There's no reason for him to stay in St. Augustine knowing that we're getting close to him. But he is, he's not running for some reason, and we need to find out why. We've missed something. If we find out what it is, we'll find him."

"We need to go over everything we've got again," EP hated to admit, but already had a vision of a stiff cup of black coffee in mind. "We'll order Chinese takeout and make it a night at the station. How's that sound?"

"It ain't crab claws but I guess it will do."

Kantz interrupted them. He had news. "Why doesn't he ever bother you?" Kidder asked Mahan before answering the telephone.

"Because I won't give him my number."

"You and Mahan need to get over to the Ramada," Kantz's tone was serious. "It's Molly Tidwell. She just told me a story that is going to knock your socks off. How soon can you get here?"

"Ten minutes," EP answered and knew

something was wrong. He had a hunch it involved Haley's father, Franklin Tidwell. "Are you about to tell me that your *gut* was right about Mr. Tidwell?"

"How'd you know?"

"What has he done?" Kidder answered the question with one of his own, rudely, but he did not notice.

"It's bad Kidder, tragic." Kantz answered craving a drink, a few drinks, what Molly had told him made his stomach hurt, and his blood boil. "I knew I should have just shot that asshole."

"Tell me Jimmy."

"He's been raping his daughter! I swear, this Haley Tidwell can't get a fuckin' break. Poor girl is probably better off dead!"

*

"So, have we been looking at this all wrong? Is there a possibility that Franklin Tidwell killed his daughter all along?" The possibility was remote, EP knew, but given the new facts, he had to believe anything was possible, just like he continued believing in the department, believing one day to find coffee grounds that did not taste like cardboard. He stared into the hot liquid with disgust, but continued. "Maybe he found out she was going to tell everybody what he'd done to her? Maybe he snapped, decided to shut her up? Wouldn't be the first time, definitely motive."

"He might have sexually abused his daughter, but I don't think he had anything to do with her disappearance," Mahan reminded Kidder they had excluded him as a suspect. Franklin's whereabouts had been accounted for when Haley went missing. He'd been at the *Fort*, watching the fireworks with his wife and the boyfriend, Jesse Moss. And he had been with Molly before that, after Haley's fight with her boyfriend, after she stormed out of the room and was never heard from again.

"And we know that Kinsinger had something to do with this. He's running for some reason. We know he was at the Ramada, under the name *Ted Cundy*. We know he's rented every movie available on serial killers, and we know in at least three of the previous cases, an alias was used resembling a serial killer, and all pertaining to movie titles that he rented. We also know that he got rid of everything in his spare bedroom, and cleaned it entirely. And he knows how to make homemade chloroform." Mahan needed a moment to breathe, but she wasn't finished. "We got two possible eye witnesses that saw him in the parking lot that night dragging a suitcase, and we have the receptionist who remembers him being there. We know his mother died in an *accidental* fire on the Fourth of July, and that his father abandoned him on the same day years prior. We know he never left a paper trail of any kind, and most of all we know that he torched his car, killed two other people and tossed their bodies inside before stealing their car. He then parked their car right in our parking lot and led us on this wild goose chase by using one of their cell phones. That's what we know EP, in a nutshell, and there's no way Franklin Tidwell was a part of any of that. He might be sick in the head, but he didn't do this."

"I bet he was watching the whole scene this afternoon, when we pulled that cab over. I bet he saw everything." EP stated referring to Abraham.

"It won't be long now," Mahan sensed if a cigarette was offered to her, she would smoke it, although she preferred a skinny joint. The stress was mounting. But they were getting close, she thought, they were right on top of him. And Kinsinger was not running. She knew that would make him easier to catch.

They hoped Molly Tidwell would know something. They needed more help.

*

Killing someone is kind of like losing your virginity. You never forget your first. Just like the bond between two people engaging in the rigorous activity of sexual penetration, it is somewhat the same when stealing someone's last breath. The best is when you kill someone at the exact moment of orgasm. I'm telling you, there is nothing like it in the world.

Want to bungee jump off a bridge? Go ahead. Want to skydive? Have at it.

How about attach jumper cables to your car battery, turn it on, and then attach the other end to your testicles? Huh. Interesting, actually.

Want to defuse a bomb? Yeah right.

How about be a hero, save a department store full of people from a band of Jihad bringing terrorists, at Christmas time…like Bruce Willis in **Die Hard***? Don't we all…*

I can guarantee you one thing, none of the adrenaline rushes experienced above can come close to taking someone's life. To hear them beg for mercy, to ignore it, to feel them fight for life, only to destroy it. To take the most precious thing away from someone, to make them realize they are about to die, watch them give up, and then feel the spirit leave their body, when everything goes silent, and still. My friends, there is simply nothing like it.

"We are who we are." I heard a lot of people say this over the years, but I accepted it as solid, grounded

advice. There was no reason for me to change, I still don't think I have done anything wrong.

I wouldn't have been able to stop anyway.

This is who I am, who I was meant to be.

Without people like me, there wouldn't be people like many of you. There would be nothing to be afraid of, nothing to teach your kids, nothing to write about, and nothing to do with your spare time.

And I consider myself lucky, that I am not like anybody else.

Unique.

I'm not afraid to explore my dark side, while all of you have to sit there, live your whole life, and wonder what it feels like. And you can't lie to me. Everyone has the ability to do things, horrible things, to other human beings. I'd even be willing to bet that everyone has thought about it. Haven't you?

Well, I'm a doer!

I can't be sorry about that.

I have absolutely no regrets.

Corrigan Mularkey, Heather Geeker, Peighton Mercer, Cassie Povia, Sally Bay Fields, and Haley Tidwell have all been the icing on top of the cake. I ravaged them, exploited them, and did things to them that no one will ever be able to understand, or want to. God they felt good. I needed them to scream. I wanted them to cry, bleed, and fear me.

I never wanted them to give up.

I would keep them around as long as they wanted to live, as long as they fought me, showed me their life meant something.

But they all eventually gave up.

That's when I would have to tell them goodbye.

I must admit, it was sad at times, but to be honest, torture just isn't the same when the one you're doing it to isn't screaming, or clawing at your flesh.

Once they stopped fighting, I stopped caring.

I was more pissed that I couldn't get an erection anymore when this happened.

And discarding of them was easy, much like taking out the garbage.

I have a graveyard actually, I might write about it later. It holds all my secrets, houses my ghosts, my shattered souls.

I did throw a couple in the river though, just to throw the police off.

Though, in all honesty, I never really felt threatened by them.

And I know you probably want to stop reading my diary at this point, but don't, not everyone is going to be as lucky as you. Like many others before you, you are getting access to my mind, and I'm giving you the answers to what I'm sure is the most prudent question of all, why?

But as you continue reading, just know one thing, you're different from all the others that have met me.

If you're lucky enough to be reading this, unlike all the others, you'll probably be able to walk away.

I did say probably, right?

*

Mahan listened to Molly Tidwell's appalling story with sorrowful ears. *Her daughter was missing, probably dead*, she thought but kept it inside, and masked those thoughts with concern filled eyes. *And then to find out that her husband had been sexually abusing her. Who could have seen this coming?* She also knew without Haley there to confirm the story, it was going to be hard to prove.

Unless Haley Tidwell was alive, and willing to

testify, chances were slim that anything could be done to punish her father, Franklin Tidwell.

"Mrs. Tidwell," Kidder spoke softly from his heart, and knelt beside the distraught woman on the hotel bed. "Do you know where your husband is now?"

"No," Molly answered, she could not stop crying, and all color had drained from her face. "He met some guy in the bar the other night when he was drunk. Said his name was Angel, or Angelo, or something like that. Anyway, he just grabbed the keys a few hours ago and said he was going out. I didn't ask where, asshole wouldn't have told me anyway."

"And he's driving the car that you guys own?"

"Yeah, it's a 2004 red Ford Expedition." Molly sniffled, arched her back, and then remembered something. "Angelo Richards, that's his name. That's the name of the guy Frank went out with."

"Hang on a second," Mahan interrupted, and she exited the room and walked to their car in parking lot, it was more of a sprint, really. She grabbed the file from the video store and returned to the room in less than two minutes. She was sweating a little, the sun had begun to set, but the humidity remained unfathomed. She did not notice. It took her a moment to find what she was looking for, but she made the connection easily. She looked towards Molly. "You say he went out with a man named Angelo Richards?"

"That's right," Molly answered, alertly, knew something important had happened. "Is something wrong?"

Mahan did not mean to, but she ignored the question and turned towards Kidder. "Can I see you outside for a second?" Kantz stayed behind with Molly as the two of them exited the room. EP noticed the worry in Mahan's eyes, and immediately asked what was wrong. "This is not good," Mahan answered and showed Kidder the file from the video store. She brought out a pen and circled a name on the page showing the list of videos Abraham Kinsinger had rented.

RICHARD ANGELO.

"Are you telling me what I think you're telling me?" EP asked, and for a brief second looked puzzled. He was not expecting this.

"Yes," Mahan's heart fluttered, she knew they had to move fast. "Abraham Kinsinger has gone after Franklin Tidwell. I don't know why, none of this is making sense right now, but this is definitely not a coincidence. I'm afraid we're too late."

"Molly shouldn't be left alone tonight," EP opened the door and motioned for Tuesday to join them. He asked if he would mind staying the night with Molly Tidwell, and Kantz agreed. "There's a chance they might come back. I need you here incase they do."

"There's more," Mahan told EP as they started down the stairs. "Richard Angelo, the name that Kinsinger is using now, well…"

"What? What is it?"

"His nickname, Richard Angelo's nickname disturbs me."

"Why?"

"Because he's known as the *Angel of Death!*"

<u>20</u>

"He's got a gun." They had been in the car for ten minutes. Both were talking on cell phones, working the case, searching for evidence, for leads. At this point, anything would do and Mahan cut her conversation short as she heard Kidder's statement. "Barry McElroy's mother just phoned the station, said he has a gun, 9 mm. Knows for a fact he took it with him camping. She had actually insisted on it."

"And let me guess, crime scene guys haven't found a gun in the torched car or the Honda CRV have they?" EP shook his head and his phone vibrated. He had a text message waiting from the reporter, Miranda Richardson. "So we have to assume that Kinsinger has the gun. As if this asshole isn't dangerous enough." EP nodded this time, and placed his knee against the steering wheel as he began typing into his phone. Miranda had heard about the bodies at the campsite, wanted to know if it was related to the story promised to her. He told her he'd call her later, and then told Mahan what Miranda wanted. She shrugged her shoulders. "I guess I'm going to have to give her something, just to keep her at bay until we end this shit."

"Tell her the killer likes attention, and the more she writes about it, the more danger she's putting herself, and other women in. Then, tell her to go suck off her editor for cover story insurance!"

"Jesus. You really can be an asshole Kidder. Just an observation."

"I'm just tired, stressed, and ready for this to be over." He knew it was wrong, but he truly had no intention of arresting Abraham Kinsinger. If no one was around, if given the opportunity, he would shoot him, kill him, and get away with it. "I know Miranda's all right. I get along with her okay, just don't want to deal with her right now is all."

"That's what I hear…"

"What?" EP was confused. The conversation had taken off without him, or ended. He wasn't sure which was taking place, truthfully.

"That you get along with her okay….Miranda."

"You want to tell me what's going on in that head of yours Mahan?"

She did not want to, and didn't. She knew what it was though, just had trouble admitting it. *Jealousy* was biting her in the ass, for some reason, and it was not going away. Then silence fell over them again, hung over them like a rain cloud, and as they maneuvered into a parking space at the Sheriff's Department, Mahan climbed out and started up the stairs without waiting for him.

It was clear, the tension evident, both had seemingly started their menstrual cycles.

But only one knew how to handle a tampon.

*

The bar was loud, messy, overwhelmed by an odor of stale smoke and beer, though the gatherers seemingly did not notice, and a local drunken country band, *The Rebels*, worked relentlessly on stage, stringing together a set of tunes, none of which were originals, however. Arnold's Bar was not known for its great service and jovial atmosphere. Instead, it was known as a great place to get laid, get drunk, catch an STD, and chances were high that if involved in a scuffle, the man's name would most likely be Bubba. It was also infested with drugs, you could find anything you wanted, just had to ask the right person....the bartender.

"Did you get it?" Franklin Tidwell was not a fan of the place. The women were trashy, resembled a band of homeless scalawags, not his type at all, and he felt icy stares from most of the men in the establishment. He sensed they did not want him there, and he would gladly leave, as soon as they got the *blow*. "Did you get it?" He really wanted to leave.

"I got it." Abraham winked at Franklin and took a seat across from him. "Do you want to have a drink before we go?"

"Nope," Franklin stood up and prepared to exit the bar. "I want to get something to drink, but not in here. Just being in this shithole makes me feel dirty, like I'm going to leave with the plague or shingles or something." Once in the Expedition, he continued, but felt a little safer. "Please tell me the girls you have lined up don't look anything like those in the bar? I don't want to bang a street whore Angelo."

"You got nothing to worry about Frank. Trust me." But that wasn't enough, Frank wanted details, wanted the girls described to him. So Abraham delivered, described autumn hair, light freckles, angelic skin, tight asses, and perfect, delectable breasts.

Then, Frank asked for directions to the motel.

He had grown excited, could feel his penis throbbing.

He pictured the girls Angelo had lined up.

Then, he pictured his daughter.

Angelo had just described his missing daughter exactly.

Perfect, he thought, reminding himself to stop at a liquor store for booze. *I hope they look just like Haley.*

*

Kidder could feel knots in his neck. When he leaned his head backwards, he felt a sharp pain filter to the base of his neck, between the shoulder blades, and his back ached slightly, but he could deal with that. He was tired, yawning uncontrollably, and he noticed his chair squeaked as he moved around his desk. He attributed the chair as being one of the main reasons his back hurt, and decided right then that it was time to buy another one, maybe even leather, one that could clean easy, he spilt coffee a lot.

Another yawn.

He could see Mahan across the room, on her phone, probably talking to her resources back in Quantico. He saw her yawn too, then cover her mouth with a clinched fist and ran her fingers through her dark hair.

Kidder wondered if he could make it as a federal agent.

Quickly dismissed the idea.

Then wondered if he and Mahan would stay connected?

He hoped so...

A red light blinked on his office phone, there were messages waiting for him, and he dismissed them at first, decided to go over his notes, work the case again with tired eyes, but everything ran together and his vision blurred. There was nothing else to do at this point, except wait, wait for another body or for Kinsinger to mess with them again.

He had his people checking the alias Angelo Richards, and the name Richard Angelo, just to see if anything turned up, but he doubted anything would.

He had dozens of patrols, stopping by local bars, motels and hotels, all armed with pictures of Kinsinger and Franklin Tidwell.

They had the right man, he knew, but still could only play the waiting game.

Abraham Kinsinger had been his adversary all these years. He had turned St. Augustine into a hunting ground. The one to cause him sleepless nights, made him question his faith, and the one to prey on the innocent, because he himself had been denied the passages of a wholesome, grounded childhood. But at least he knew now what the face of evil looked like.

He had looked in Abraham's eyes, he would never forget them.

And if he got the opportunity to do it again, well, he was sure he would end it, he would have to, in order to sleep again.

He had to get rid of the knots in his neck too.

Finally, he threw a pile of papers on his desk and picked up the telephone, deciding it was time to check his messages. There were twelve in all.

His Captain had phoned, needed to talk, concerning the lawsuit his father had phoned him about earlier, and that could wait.

Two others, both from the state's attorney's office, needing information for another case he had worked. Those could wait too.

His Captain again, he was angry. Still, Kidder wasn't in the mood right now, and hoped his superior had gone home for the evening.

Then, there were five hang-ups. He wondered why people did that. If they knew they weren't going to leave a message, then why wait until the end of the voicemail to hang up? Why waste the time, of both parties no less?

Finally, one captured his attention.

It was from a retired detective, Andy Chandler. He had retired around four years ago, pushed out more than anything else, he thought that was accurate anyway, and then had started his own private agency. They had crossed paths a few times over the years, intersecting cases and just routine field work. Chandler had a way about him, Kidder knew, a way to always get what he wanted, willing to take risks in the process, bend the law, find the loopholes. Before he retired, his reputation inside the department had not been on the level, and some thought that Chandler had taken money, a lot of money, from his conquests. He'd even been investigated internally, suspected of covering up crimes, planting evidence, helping people get away with their mistakes, if they paid accordingly of course. He could keep a secret though; many people sought him for advice.

Nothing ever came of it though, no charges formerly brought.

But everyone knew.

In the end, when he retired, his full pension granted, all the gossip had simply gone away.

And now, for some reason, he had phoned Kidder.

The message was brief, to the point, as expected with Andy Chandler. "Detective Kidder, it's been a long time. I hope walking the line hasn't turned you into a pussy. Never saw you as a politician, you're not like your old man at all. I've always thought you were better than that anyway. Listen," Andy had paused, coughing, sounded as if he had aged ten years. "I know you're busy, and I don't want to waste your time, or cause any trouble, that's not my intent. But I've been following *your* case in papers and on the news. I know you say the guy whose picture you've been plastering everywhere, Abraham Kinsinger, is not a suspect, but I think we both know better than that, don't we Ernest? Anyway, I think you should call me back. We need to get caught up anyway. I have some information….what you do with it, however, is completely up to you. You got my number."

Two more messages.

Another hang up.

The last one did not leave a name, but Kidder recognized the voice instantly. Abraham Kinsinger had called him.

"I know you're looking for me Kidder, and I'm flattered, truly. You've been looking for me a long time, and if I were to get caught, I'd want it to be you, truly. But let's not get foolish, too ahead of ourselves. We're on two opposite sides of the spectrum, you and I, and I strongly feel it should stay that way. I'm calling to say goodbye, will be leaving soon, moving on. I'm going to try and turn my life around," he listened as Abraham chuckled benevolently, it disturbed him. "Anyway, I've been working on something for you. You'll find it sooner or later, and don't worry, you don't owe me anything. Consider it a gift, friend. Goodbye Kidder, and tell that fine piece of ass that's been helping you that I said hello."

"Motherfucker!" EP slammed the phone down on the receiver and made his way towards Mahan. *I'm going to shoot you, truly!*

He made a note to return Andy Chandler's phone call.

Now, however, even that could wait.

*

"He told me hello," Mahan pressed, all ears. She was not surprised Kinsinger had made contact though, had expected it actually. "If you don't shoot this guy I'm going to."

Kidder phoned Jimmy Kantz. "Everything quiet at the Ramada?"

"Yep, Molly's all fucked up though. I don't know if she's going to recover from this shit. No word from Frank. We've been calling him nonstop, bastard has his phone turned off."

"Yeah, we're tracking it. If he turns it on or uses it, we'll know. Stay alert though Tuesday, Kinsinger left me a message at my office. We're trying to trace that now too, Mahan and I are headed out now."

"Be careful Kidder, both these guys have major issues. Hate to think what they'll do if backed into a corner…"

"I'm more worried about what I'm going to do in that corner…."

"Let's just end this shit tonight."

*

An hour later, Abraham's call had been traced to a convenient store across the street from a well-known bar in St. Augustine, Arnold's.

The clerk didn't remember anything.

Kidder assumed Abraham had stopped there for a reason, envisioned he had passed by there on his way to somewhere close by. He looked across the street towards the bar, was well aware that nothing but bad news came in and out of that particular watering hole. He wanted to check it out anyway.

Mahan had just ended a call when he climbed back in the car, and looked his way. "It's confirmed, the bodies from the car at the campsite belong to Barry McElroy and Savannah Clayton. And everything is pointing to the car being a Buick LeSabre. That's all we need to crucify this asshole, now we just have to find him."

"Well, let's start over there," EP pointed towards the bar across the street.

"You buying a round?"

"I wish."

"I won't tell." Mahan was smitten, it showed. "Do they serve crab claws?"

"Mess around in Arnold's," EP forced a smile. "And you just might leave there with a case of *crabs*, I promise."

21

"What are you doing?" Franklin Tidwell had finished half the bottle of crown on his own, had grown antsy. The motel room was disgusting, and he lay on the bed, flipping through the yellow pages of the phonebook. He'd find live entertainment, companionship, one way or another. Abraham sat at the table by the window, cowering over something, a notebook, and he was writing something, focused, looked like he was breathing heavy. Frank noticed. "That looks like a fucking diary. Are you writing in a fucking diary Angelo?"

"Yes," Abraham was annoyed, he needed to finish it, years of work were drawing to an end, and he needed closure, it was his thing. "They'll be here soon. Just relax," he spoke of the girls he had lied about for tonight's extravaganza. There were not any girls, none were coming over. They never were. He focused on his diary again. "Leave me alone Frankie!"

I had problems before, admitting to the things I've done.

But not anymore, people know too much about me already. That's okay though, I knew my secret life would surface eventually. Granted, and I do admit, that I would rather have remained undetected for years to come, but be that as it may, things change in life, and my life is no exception.

So, let me be polite and introduce myself accordingly.

My name is Abraham Kinsinger, and I'm a serial killer.

Have been for a while, just got off to a late start. Better late than never, I guess. That's probably something my father, Henry, would have said. "Better late than never!" I would have known that if he'd stuck around, but of course, he didn't, had better things to do. But that reminds me, remember when I wrote that my father used to say "beggars can't be choosers?" I told you earlier in this diary those words, that saying, was true. But it really isn't, at least not to me. Beggars can be choosers in my eyes. As long as my victims begged for life, I'd let them live, force them to absorb more pain. As long as they begged, I chose to let them live. But as soon as the screaming stopped, I killed them.

All except one.
Haley Tidwell.
She was dead already, I just helped the process along.

*

"What is the purpose of this call Andy?" Stephen Kidder did not like being bothered at home with work, on his home phone no less, regardless of who wanted to talk to him. "Why are you calling me on my home phone anyway? Martha is just in the other room."

"I'll be blunt Mr. City Manager, I want something."

"And what just might that be?" He suspected he knew the answer.

"Money, I think five thousand should do to be exact."

"Five thousand dollars?" Stephen felt his cheeks turn a fiery red. His heart beat quickened. He knew this day might come, prayed it would not. Prayed Andy Chandler would just die. But here it was, and he had to handle it. "What makes you think I'm going to give you five thousand dollars? Are you seriously trying to blackmail a government official Chandler? What's this all about?"

"I think you know."

And he was right, Stephen Kidder did know.

*

Franklin Tidwell needed to piss, and left who he thought was a man by the name of Angelo Richards to his writing, to his laughable diary writing of all things. The two of them were about to have sex, exploit a couple of welcoming, young, tender vaginas, and all this asshole wanted to do was write in a fucking journal? As he closed the bathroom door behind him, however, he surmised there were certainly worse things to write about.

Yeah right.

"Weird motherfucker," Franklin said aloud as he started urinating in the toilet and arched his back.

He was drunk, but wanted more. He wasn't going home tonight anyway.

Then, he heard a faint voice.

Barely audible, but was sure he heard it.

He yelled for Angelo, asked if he had said anything, but there was no response. Was he being ignored? Had the girls finally arrived? His stream of urine came to a drip and he shook it violently, and then tried to cram his package back into his pants.

The voice came again.

It was clearer this time.

"Dad," the voice said softly, but cold and vengeful. "Daddy."

"What the fuck?" Franklin Tidwell was certain he was hearing things. A lot had happened over the course of the past few days, a lot had come to light, and it was possible he was losing his mind. He was alone in the bathroom, he was sure, and Angelo was in the room, on the other side of the door.

"Fuck you dad!"

The voice was loud now, and he recognized it.

"Haley, is that you?" He turned to face the bathtub, and saw the shower curtain had been drawn to a close. "Are you there?" He knew that was not possible, she had been abducted, taken by a serial killer. She was not alive, couldn't be. It was not possible.....

"I'm here dad. It's me!"

Franklin pulled the shower curtain back and only had a second to take in the sight of his daughter.

Haley lunged at him with an evil grin.

He noticed her bruises, her cuts, the pale skin, and knew this was not the girl he had raised, figured Angelo had done this to her, had planned this all along. He thought all of this in a matter of seconds, and still could not react.

Haley's legs wrapped around him and pulled him close.

She had a cloth, laced with the chloroform Abraham had made for her, and forced it into his mouth and over his nose.

Haley was straddling her father on the toilet when darkness consumed him.

Then, she opened the bathroom door and found Abraham smiling at her on the edge of the bed in the motel room.

"I did it," she breathed, shaking

"How do you feel?" he asked passionately, with an erection, and brushed past her into the bathroom to view the limp body of Franklin Tidwell. He had never used chloroform on a male before, and wanted to work fast, before it wore off. "Was it how I told you it was going to be?"

"Yes," Haley felt a rush come over, something she had never felt before. "I feel good!"

"Then you're really going like what happens next."

22

The terrain of Twelve Mile Swamp never changed this time of year.
It rained a lot in Florida during the summer months, damn near everyday, sometimes only a quick downpour pushed through the area, and other days, mother-nature presented the state with a day-long event. Regardless, it seemed like it rained everyday and that kept the ground somewhat mushy, slippery, but Abraham was used to it. And he would help Haley out if she needed it, though he doubted she would.
Luckily, today's shower had been over in ten minutes, and the heat and humidity and helped solidify the ground beneath his feet.
They were only a mile away from his home, risky, he knew, but he had promised to show Haley everything.
They parked at the entrance, looked down the street, no signs of life, or trouble. She helped him remove her unconscious father from the back of the Expedition and drug him into the brush. Then, he told Haley to stay with her father, gave her the gun, the Ruger 9 mm, and more chloroform, and he proceeded to drive the SUV down the street. There really wasn't a place to hide it, but Abraham knew they would be looking for it, he was sure they knew *Angelo Richards* was with Franklin Tidwell by now. Leaving the car at the entrance to the swamp was not a good idea.
So, Abraham drove it down the road, probably a half mile, away from any houses, and then veered

left, into the woods, as far as he could go. He parked it at least ten feet into the woods, centered between a couple of trees and now flattened bushes. The streetlights were dim, and that helped. No one would see it without a spotlight, unless they were looking for it.

And the *piggies* were, he knew.

Then, he ran back down the road, dodged into the brush every time he saw headlights coming towards or behind him.

No one saw him.

When he finally made it back to Haley, Franklin was still unconscious.

"Now what?" Haley asked, and handed the gun back to Abraham.

"Now, we set you free Haley. Now we make sure he can never hurt you again."

They each grabbed an arm, pulled Franklin Tidwell to his feet, and then slowly began dragging him deeper into the swampland.

Deeper into Abraham Kinsinger's graveyard……..

*

Mahan was sure she would never go back to Arnold's, ever, not even if her life depended on it.

And crab claws were not even on the menu.

"Told you so," EP laughed as they climbed in his Tahoe and pulled out of the parking lot. Regardless, the bartender had confirmed their suspicions, both Franklin Tidwell and Abraham Kinsinger had been there, about and hour or two ago, apparently only for a couple of minutes and then left. The bartender had seen Kinsinger there plenty of times before, but admitted that Tidwell looked out of place, sensed trouble and was glad to see them leave.

"Wonder what those mongrels would have done to Tidwell is they stayed?" Mahan was curious, a bit horny.

"You don't want to know." Then EP's phone vibrated and he answered it without looking at who was calling. "This is Kidder."

"Got a positive ID on Kinsinger and Tidwell. They were seen by the front desk attendant at a rundown motel off Ponce de Leon." The officer sounded excited, wanted encouragement. "I'm here now. The room is empty. No sign of either man. There's nothing here."

EP did not give encouragement, a lecture instead. "Get the fuck out of the room and don't touch anything. I'm on my way. You should have contacted me as soon as you confirmed Kinsinger was there. Never, ever go into a situation like that without backup. Do you understand?"

"Yes sir. I apologize. I was just trying to-"

EP cut him off. "Don't apologize, and don't *try* to do anything. Just get the fuck out of the room and don't let anyone else inside."

His wit's end had finally crept up on him.

*

"How long until he wakes up?" Haley was anxious, nervous, but determined at the same time. Her father was tied to a pine tree, immobilized by a roll of duct tape, one of its many uses. He was not going anywhere, could not hurt her, or Abraham, but the thrill of the moment had seized her, and she was ready to get on with it.

"Anytime now." Abraham was thankful for the full moon, he did notice a flashlight in the Expedition, but forgot to grab it. That was okay, it only took a little while for his eyes to get adjusted to the dim lighting anyway. He walked over and slapped Franklin Tidwell across the face.

Nothing.

He slapped him again, and again.

There was movement, then a moan, and then their captive's head started rocking back and forth, saliva spilled from the center of Frank's mouth. Haley cowered away at the sight of her father's movement, at the blinking of his eyes, but Abraham pulled her back. "Don't be afraid," he said, still turned on, and rubbed her back. "Let him see you. Let him know what you're about to do."

"I can't," Haley's voice was soft, and crackling, but believable. She knew she could do it, though, knew she lied.

"I want you right now," Abraham said as Franklin tried to move, realized he was tied to a tree.

"No," Haley stepped away from his grasp and asked for the knife.

Abraham gave it to her.

"Haley, is that you?" Frank's tone was low, it felt as if he had been sleeping for days, and visions of the bathroom in the motel room resurfaced. He saw *Angelo* in the background, tried to understand. "Baby, its daddy. Are you okay? Untie me from this tree sweetheart. Let me take you home."

"You took me away from my home a long time ago," Haley seemed ready, moved in close, and pressed the illuminate silver blade against his throat. "When you decided to put your dick inside me, you took me away from my home. My home is Abraham now."

"You mean Angelo?"

"She means Abraham." He took control as he

moved in, and took the knife from Haley's hands. "I'm the one that took your daughter Frankie. But she told me what you did to her, she told me everything."

"You motherfucker!" Franklin squirmed, but could not move. He was paralyzed. He spat, snarled, and clawed at the ground with the tips of his fingernails.

Abraham laughed, and then howled like a coyote into the night. "They always fight," he said, loving the moment. "They always do this." Then, he looked into Haley's eyes and remembered. "Except you Haley. You didn't fight me at all."

Then, he showed Haley where to cut her father. How to kill him.

And she did.

"Please don't," Franklin pleaded as the knife entered his stomach. But it was no use, Haley pulled the knife out and stabbed him again, sank the blade into his flesh as far as it would go. Then again, and again until she was sure he was gurgling on his own blood.

"Yes," Abraham felt rejuvenated. "That's it." Then he ripped off his shirt and slung Haley to the ground. His pants were unbuttoned seconds later, and he looked back at Franklin, barely alive, but was, and watching. "Let him watch me fuck you. I want to be inside you right now."

"Okay," Haley agreed and let the knife slip from her fingertips. Insects were chirping, and mosquitoes biting, but it did not matter. Nothing did. He climbed on top of her at first, and then flipped her over, so that she was on all fours and thrust himself inside her. Her mouth was open, and her eyes glistened in ecstasy. Her moaning filtered out the night noise, and she glared into her father's eyes as

Abraham slammed her back and forth. All creatures of the night were silent, in awe of the spectacle around them.

Abraham watched Franklin Tidwell's fingertips as he screwed his daughter right in front of him.

His hands were still clawing at the ground.

He was still dying....

*

When the orgasms came, Haley Tidwell realized she had never felt that before. Not with Jesse Moss, not with any of her other partners. She also realized she liked what she felt, wanted to feel it again.

Abraham lied next her, staring at the moon, expressionless.

"Do you always feel like this afterwards?" She asked coldly, and gazed into the eyes of her dead father. Abraham nodded, he did not want to speak, didn't want to ruin the moment. She pulled up her pants and walked close to him, knelt beside the tree and put her ear close to her father's mouth, wiping the knife clean of her fingerprints with his shirt.

He wasn't breathing.

But that didn't mean he was dead.

"Is he dead?" she asked Abraham, determined to destroy his reverie.

"I hope not."

"Why?"

"Because I wanted him to see everything, wanted him to feel me inside you." Then, Abraham climbed to his feet and picked up the knife. He pushed Haley out of the way and knelt beside Franklin Tidwell.

He did not know if he was dead or not.

But he gashed his throat anyway, and then pinned him to the tree by steering the blade of the knife right through his sliced neck.

"If he wasn't dead, he is now."

Haley saw the gun on the ground and went for it, and Abraham did not try to stop her, didn't sense any danger.

But with the gun in hand, she pointed it at his chest, and warned him not to move.

"I don't understand Haley," Abraham smiled, crouched, like a tiger, but did not move. "I gave you everything you wanted, I made you see who you really are. You don't need that gun. I am not going to hurt you."

"I'm sorry," Haley started weeping and tried to focus. She had learned a lot from Abraham over the course of her captivity, including how to get away with murder.

He was now her only witness.

And as he would have said, she could not have that.

"Think about what you're doing," Abraham pleaded, realizing what was about to happen. "I'm sorry it had to be you, I'm sor-"

The sound of the gun startled him, as it did the wildlife. The wings of birds flapped in the distance, searching for cover.

But Abraham never screamed.

He looked at his chest, touched it, felt blood gushing from the open wound, and found it hard to breathe.

"I don't understand," he spoke softly, and fell to his knees as his vision blurred.

"I'm sorry," Haley repeated, dropping the gun and prepared to walk away. She had been careful to remember the way out of the swamp, even asked

Abraham where her father's Expedition was parked. He had told her, trusted her, and never sensed the plan that had been forming in her head. "But my father hurt me, and so did you. I have to make sure no one ever hurts me again." Then, she took the keys from his pocket, and started walking away, into the moonlight, and never looked back.

Abraham watched her shadow disappear, listened to her footsteps as the brush crunched beneath her feet.

And as her silhouette evaporated, his struggle to breathe continued.

He remembered the feeling that had been tormenting him over the past few days, thought about it clearly now.

Now, he was sure.
He had fallen in love.
Never felt that before.
No one had ever loved him.

*

Haley found the spot where Abraham had parked her father's car and climbed inside.

The key worked, the engine sprang to life.

Life, she thought as she backed out onto Lewis Speedway and started towards the Ramada. She knew her mother was going to be glad to see her. *Life,* she thought again. *Life is so fucking sweet!*

She started laughing, but truly wanted to cry.

23

Jimmy Kantz welcomed EP and Mahan into the motel room at the Ramada. Molly Tidwell was in the bathroom, freshening up, trying not to look like death, but smelled worse, to the point where she did not recognize her reflection in the mirror anymore. "Things are heating up," she heard Kidder's voice, had turned the water off and listened through the door. "He's trying to make this personal with me?" Molly assumed EP was speaking of Abraham Kinsinger. *Had they found her husband's body?* She hoped so.

Then, Molly exited the bathroom.

Mahan observed the frail nature and demeanor of Molly Tidwell and believed Tuesday's inference earlier. She did not look good, unhealthy, on edge, and Mahan too, now had her doubts. There was definitely a chance Molly would not make it through this.

Tragic, but Mahan had seen this before.

There were support groups, sure, and therapists, even certain drugs were helpful. There were literally thousands of people with degrees, willing to help, pretending to understand, and pretending to care.

But no one ever truly heals; Mahan was sure, after going through something like Molly Tidwell.

In every one of these cases, an empty void remains that can never be filled.

"Anything going on?"

EP nodded, told her Abraham had left him a voicemail. Told her they had traced the call to a convenient store, and then confirmed that both her husband and Abraham had been seen together at the bar. There was not much more to tell, but EP did explain they were hopeful Abraham would call again, and still hoped Franklin would turn up alive. Franklin was bigger than Abraham, noticeably taller and stronger, and EP knew that he had never gone after a male before.

"What are the chances," Molly breathed, and grabbed a 7up from the small refrigerator in the hotel room. "Of Franklin making friends with the man suspected of kidnapping Haley?"

"There is no chance." Mahan did not believe in coincidences. Certainly did not want Molly Tidwell to be misled. She needed the truth, deserved nothing less. "Your husband and Abraham did not meet by chance. This was planned, he's probably been watching the two of you since he abducted your daughter."

Tuesday moved in and offered Molly a Kleenex just as a wave of tears began to flow. "It's okay Mrs. Tidwell. We aren't going to rest until we find this guy. We're getting close."

"And my daughter, is there a chance she's still alive?"

None of them answered, none willing to field the question.

Mahan walked outside with EP and leaned against the railing on the second floor, stared at the parking lot below, the lines in the asphalt needed to be repainted, she noticed, she noticed everything.

"You okay?" EP asked, nudging her shoulder, still irritable.

"Something just isn't sitting right with me. It doesn't make any sense for Abraham to go after Franklin Tidwell. He targets women, young, defenseless women. He rapes them, tortures them, and keeps them chained to beds. It's just not his style. Frank does not meet the profile..."

"Maybe he started caring about Haley?"

Mahan thought about that, figured it had to be a possibility, but was still leaning towards dismissing the idea. "I suppose anything is possible," she said. "But I've never heard of a serial killer growing a conscience. These men act on impulses, and some of those impulses, many would testify, can not be controlled. If he abducted Haley, he would be compelled to kill her, just as he was compelled to take her in the first place. I'm certain, however, these impulses would not have applied to Franklin Tidwell."

"What about this," EP leaned in, their shoulders square with one another. Mahan felt his breath on her, could smell him again. She wanted to run her fingers through his curly black hair again. EP continued. "Say he kidnaps Haley, takes her home, starts raping her, beating her, whatever. Let's assume he finds out about what her father did to her, don't you think that could possibly change him?"

"Go on," Mahan was amused.

"Think about it. I mean Kinsinger's childhood was fucked up to say the least. Never had a father, to speak of, and watched his mom die in a fire, on the Fourth of July no less. But let's just say you were right, when you questioned whether that fire was an accident or not. What if it wasn't? What if Abraham started that fire that night, killing his mother intentionally?"

"Then we'd have to ask the question, why?"

"Hear me out," EP was on a roll, everything was working overtime inside his head, on caffeine and adrenaline. "Good question, why would he kill his mother? What if she did things to him, sexually abused him, just like what Haley's father did to her?"

"We can't prove that."

"No but it makes perfect sense. It's logical if you think about it. I think we're trying to make this too confusing."

"If he calls you again, you should ask him," Mahan suggested, admitted that Kidder's theory had merit, made sense. "You should catch him off guard and bombard him with questions about his mother, see if he blinks?"

"Oh he'll blink," EP was not done. "Think about it, if he learned that the same thing happened to Haley that had happened to him, he would view her differently, he wouldn't see her like all the others. He'd probably start feeling sorry for her, probably start remembering his own pain, and remember his mother. He would have to project his anger on someone, the person who is responsible for his pain, Haley's pain. And that person is Franklin Tidwell."

"Okay. But if that's true, then what did he do with Haley?"

"What do you mean?"

"If he started viewing Haley as a person, someone like him, if he did start feeling sorry for her and wanted to kill her father, then what did he do with her? If he started seeing her as an equal, his impulses would have changed, I don't think he would have been able to kill her at that point. It would have seemed wrong, he would start feeling like his mother, and he wouldn't want that."

EP was stuck. "You think there's a chance that Haley Tidwell is still alive?"

"If you're right about what's happened," Mahan smiled and reached over to nudge his shoulder. She hit him harder than he had hit her, on purpose of course. "If you're right, I know she's alive."

"But then that changes things."

"It also raises a lot more questions," Mahan was skeptical.

"I don't know," EP smiled and turned to walk back inside the hotel room. "Maybe you're right about all that impulse shit."

"Why do you say that?"

"Because I've been having a hard time controlling mine lately."

"Need any help?"

*

Jimmy "*Tuesday*" Kantz was on the phone when they entered, on his feet, pacing the room, Molly looked dumbfounded, they even detected a hint of joy, perhaps a glimmer of hope. "Are you fucking sure it's her?" He paused and waited for the officer on the other end of the line to continue, he shook his head up and down and clinched his fists passionately. "I can't fucking believe it. Stay where you are officer, we're on our way. Good fucking job kid," he added before hanging up. Then, he looked at Mahan and EP, pulled Molly Tidwell to her feet and hugged her. "I got good news, your daughter is alive!"

Molly trembled in ecstasy, would have collapsed if Kantz was not holding her up.

"No way," Kidder began, questions already mounting. "Where is she?"

"Patrol officer saw a red Ford Expedition matching our description driving down Ponce de Leon and pulled it over. He found Haley behind the wheel," Kantz paused and looked directly into Molly's eyes. He wanted Molly to listen to what he said next. "She was heading here, she was coming to see you Molly, coming home to her mother."

"Oh my baby! My poor baby…I've got to get to her, she needs me."

"I'll take you."

There was a sigh of relief in the room, along with a sudden silence.

They were all smiling.

But there were still a lot of questions.

Questions only Haley Tidwell could answer.

Where was Abraham Kinsinger?
Where was her father?
How had she gotten away?

*

Molly rode with Kantz, Mahan and EP followed behind.

Something stirred in Mahan's mind, something still bothered her, even though the girl they had been looking for had apparently made it home alive. Still, the feelings of complete rejoice remained absent. *Maybe I'm just tired*, she thought. More times than not, she remembered, her journey always ended standing over another corpse. Happy endings were very seldom, almost nonexistent.

Kidder was troubled too.

But he couldn't put his finger on it.

He thought about Mahan, what she had said moments ago.

Her thoughts intrigued him.

Impulses, he thought. *Did Abraham Kinsinger really let Haley go? Impulses, impulses, impulses. Would he have really just let her drive away? And what about her father, had she seen him, seen what Abraham was going to do to him? Impulses, impulses. Would Haley have wanted Abraham to hurt her father? Would she have wanted to? Impulses, impulses, impulses.*

Would she have helped him, would he have forced her too?

Impulses, impulses, impulses, fucking IMPULSES!

*

Stephen Kidder phoned EP as they arrived to the scene.

EP confirmed the girl was alive, admitted they still did not have Abraham in custody, and that Franklin Tidwell was still missing. He promised to call back as soon as he had more news, told him he would question the girl as soon as she felt up to it, after the doctors said she was okay.

Haley was already in the back of an ambulance as EP and Mahan climbed out of the car.

They noticed the reporter, Miranda Richardson, standing near by. "Fuckin' media!" Kidder waved at the redhead, but then growled as he turned his back on her and continued on his way. He told a few passing uniformed officers to make sure no one from the media got close to the Expedition, or the girl.

"You should be happy," Mahan sounded enthusiastic, yet her tone was also laced with sarcasm. "I can see the headlines now. Kidder SAVES WOMAN FROM SERIAL KILLER! LOCAL HERO COMES THROUGH!"

EP ignored her. "How is she?" He asked a paramedic, caught a glimpse of Haley from where he stood. She did not look good, her skin looked black and blue, bruised all over, and it looked as if she'd been cut more then two dozen times, though most scabs showed signs of healing.

Haley was crying, holding her mother, their

eyes met.

EP offered an encouraging smile, she returned it.

"Her vitals are good," the paramedic answered. "We're taking her to the hospital now. "But poor girl looks like she's been put through pure hell. I think she's going to be okay, but she's going to need therapy if you ask me. No way a person goes through something like that and......"

EP understood, told him they'd be following them to the hospital.

Then, back in the car, he finished the paramedic's sentence. Mahan tried to follow. "No way a person goes through something like that and doesn't get fucked up."

Abraham Kinsinger went through *it* with his mother, it fucked him up.

And now, Haley Tidwell had gone through *it*.

Twice, first *it* had been with her father, and then with Abraham Kinsinger.

Had *it* fucked her up?

Kidder needed her to answer questions as soon as possible. They could not wait any longer. If she knew where Abraham was, or her father, they had to find them, and fast.

"You know what I think," Mahan had grabbed his hand again, squeezed it gently. "I think *you're* fucked up!"

*

Doctors tried to keep Kidder out of the room. They tried.

"More lives might be in danger," he had told them, leaned in to them as he would a criminal. "That girl could help us save lives. You want it on your conscience if someone else goes missing, if someone else dies?"

"She's been through a traumatic experience," they continued to fight him. "And we got a female nurse on the way to do a rape kit."

"I'll be gentle."

"You got ten minutes and then you have to leave."

*

Molly smiled as Mahan and EP entered the hospital room.

Haley had her head down, in her mother's lap. She felt their presence, and sat up.

"These are two of the people who worked night and day trying to find you sweetheart," Molly spoke softly, assured her daughter that they were okay, could be trusted. Then they introduced themselves, told them why they were there, and the importance of the questions they needed to ask. They knew some of the questions were going to be hard to answer, hated to ask them, but they needed Haley's help, they needed closure. They needed to find Abraham Kinsinger. "Are you sure this can't wait until morning? She's been through so much already...."

Mahan and EP understood Molly's skepticism. But they had no choice.

"We'll only be ten minutes...."

"Its okay mom," Haley spoke after clearing her throat and wiping her eyes. The makeup she had been wearing on the night of the Fourth had long since worn off, and the last of her tears were sniffled away. "I can handle it...if they really need my help?"

"We do," Mahan smiled at the twenty-three

year old girl in front of her, ecstatic she had survived. "We truly need your help."

"You want to know about Abraham don't you?"

EP nodded, shocked at Haley's forwardness, noticed coldness in her voice when she mentioned Abraham's name.

"Do you know where he is?" Mahan asked.

"Yes, I can show you. I shot him, that's how I got away."

"You shot Abraham Kinsinger?" Kidder questioned, wondered how her mood could have changed suddenly.

"Yes, I had to." Haley noticed the skepticism in Kidder's eyes, like she was inside his head. It took her a few tries, but she forced herself to cry again, and again, until the stream was fluent, her eyes blurred. "He killed my father, and he was about to kill me. I'm sorry, I had to shoot him…..I had too."

"Haley, sweetheart," Mahan knelt in front of the distraught girl, saw her reflection in the girl's tears. "It's okay. We know what your father did to you, we know everything."

"You know?" Haley had not expected this. How did they know about what her father did to her? She looked at her mother, confused. Had her father told her about it? Had she told the police? She had never told anyone about her father, no one except Abraham. Still, she had to keep the act up, she could not let them see through her. "It was a long time ago…"

"Ssshhh," Mahan rubbed the girl's leg. "You don't have to talk about that right now sweetheart. But we do need you to take us to Abraham if that's okay? Can you do that for us? After that, the rest of our questions can wait until the morning. Okay?"

Haley nodded, still crying.

Have I made any mistakes?

She was sure she did not. Abraham had taught her well.

She was glad the questions were going to wait until the morning though, she had some thinking to do.

So did Kidder.

He explained to the doctors where they were taking Haley, and promised to bring her right back.

He was still thinking when they climbed in the car.

More so, when they pulled onto Lewis Speedway, and parked in front of the entrance to Twelve Mile Swamp.

His thoughts buried him as they turned on flashlights and entered the conservation area.

Fuckin' impulses.

24

Frank's body was there, his throat cut, he had bled out, and the crimson fuel had formed puddles all around him. He had at least six other stab wounds to his midsection, and duct taped to a large pine tree. Kidder was certain he had suffered, dearly, and as he looked back towards Haley, surrounded by the loving arms of her mother, Molly, both escorted by Tuesday, he noticed a heavy amount of blood spatter along her clothes and skin.

Was it her blood?

Her father's?

She had shot Abraham in the chest, was it his blood?

And where was Abraham Kinsinger? There was a pool of blood ten feet away from Franklin Tidwell's body, Kidder was kneeling next to it now, and he saw footprints, leading deeper into the swamp, and more drops of blood, but there was no sign of Abraham.

EP needed answers and walked towards Haley, she looked up at him with angelic eyes. "Are you sure you shot him?" She confirmed with a nod. "And he went down?"

"Yes. I shot him in the chest, right where you were standing. I ran to my father, tried to help him, but he was dead, so, I…..I just ran away. I'm sorry, I didn't know what else to do."

Well that explains the blood on her clothes, EP thought.

"I think that's enough questions for now Detective Kidder," Molly had regained her composure, her motherly stature. "I think we should get her back to the hospital. Maybe she'll feel up to talking more tomorrow." EP's eyes met Jimmy's, they nodded to one another and then he watched as his partner began escorting mother and daughter back through the swamp, towards safety, towards the end of the nightmare.

"We got a knife over here!" An officer yelled, and held it high with a pair of latex laden hands. He was standing near Franklin Tidwell.

"Bag it," Kidder responded. "Get it to the lab, I want prints!" Then, he got on his cell phone and dialed dispatch. He motioned for Mahan to join him, he wanted to follow the blood trail. If Kinsinger was wounded the way Haley described, he could not get far. He would bleed out, or drown.... "Listen up everyone," he spoke into the phone and to the search team. "I want all hands on deck on this one. I want all radios switched to channel three, and I want you all to split up in pairs of two. I want every available chopper with a spotlight to start searching the area, and I want the rest of us to split up, and cover every inch of this swamp, let's go with a three mile square radius. I also want every available K9 unit in route ASAP. Suspect is shot, chest wound, he could not have gotten far. And be careful, he is armed and dangerous. Let's go people!"

"You ready for this?" Mahan asked as she fell in behind Kidder where the blood trail began.

"Just stay behind me, keep your eyes peeled. We'll shoot first, answer questions later."

The blood trail was frequent at first, and then stopped completely about fifty yards into the swamp.

They heard the blades of the helicopters cutting through the dead air, followed what they thought were footsteps through thick muck and slippery wetland, but they could not be sure.

The search went on all night.

It continued all day the next day.

And in the end, the only body removed from the swamp had been that of Franklin Tidwell.

They did not find the gun, either.

Abraham Kinsinger had simply disappeared.

"I don't understand. He could not have gotten far!" Kidder was furious, wanted to go home. "If she shot him where she said she did, he would have had trouble breathing, blood might have even started collecting in his lungs. He could not have made it far."

"Have we checked the hospitals for gun shot wounds?"

"Yes, I even got a tail on Miguel Hampton. He would help him if he had the chance. I know he warned Abraham we were coming that day. Something isn't right here, no way he made it out of there alive."

"Maybe he didn't," Mahan suggested, wanting to believe it herself, but simply was not sure. "Maybe he's dead somewhere out there, maybe he's in the mud, waiting to be mauled by animals." Not likely. "If he's out there, we'll find his body. And if he made it out, he'd have to get that wound checked out immediately in order to survive."

"That's a lot of maybe's agent Pierce!"

"Well right now, that's all I got!"

"We need to talk to the girl again."

"We need some coffee and a change of clothes......"

*

Haley answered all their questions an hour later.

She explained everything.

How she came to meet Abraham on the night of the Fourth of July, how he'd snuck up behind her, how she never had a chance. She told them what he did to her, chained to the bed, the rape sessions, the beatings, everything. She told them how he had changed when she mentioned what her father had done to her, how he snapped, told her he was going to kill her father, and was going to make her watch. She explained how he had taken her to another motel room, one with a small amount of human traffic, and how he had threatened her, told her if she tried to run away, or call the police, that he would kill her mother also. She told them she did not want to obey him, but felt she had to, she did not want anything to happen to her mother, she would not have been able to live with that on her conscience.

Most of what she told them was lies.

But they believed her, she knew, believed everything she said. And why wouldn't they, she had the scars, the cuts, the bruises, and Abraham's semen inside of her. She had enough evidence to back her story up, to give her credibility.

They had no choice but to believe her.

Even how the blood appeared on her clothes and skin, they even found some under her fingernails.

She explained that too.

She told them she ran to her father after shooting Abraham, had hugged him, and tried to put pressure on the wounds. How when she watched him die, helplessness took over her mind.

She cried throughout most of the questioning.

That had been easy.

But when they told her they had not found Abraham's body, that they were not sure he was dead, she looked concerned, genuinely scared, and she was.

She had gained his trust, only to turn on him.

If he was alive, she knew, he would come after her.

Sooner or later, she was sure, he would find her, and finish what he started.......

As for now, though, her mom wanted to take her home, back to Tallahassee, both wanting a fresh start, both needing to put the past behind them.

Her mom had promised a "for sale" sign would be hung in the lawn immediately. She would call a realtor, and pursue a *quick sale*. Haley smiled at the thought of a new life.

She also smiled at the thought of her ex-boyfriend, Jesse Moss.

She wanted to see him.

Wanted to teach him a lesson.

He should have never cheated on me with my best friend!

And she knew how to hide his body, dispose of it, Abraham had taught her well, told her everything.

She just had to find the perfect spot, though.

Creating a graveyard of her own would be fun.

Filling it with bodies would be fun, too.

She laughed inside, she could not stop. All the while, an assortment of magical tears fell from her face.

"It's going to be ok sweetheart," her mother imposed, wiped the tears from her face with a tissue. "Everything is going to be fine."

Yes. You have no idea...

*

Kidder felt like he had slept for two solid days.

Still, he did not feel rested, more tired truthfully, but he knew he had to get back to reality.

It was noon when he took his first sip of coffee, and he checked his phone.

Mahan had called him three times, she was leaving in the afternoon, and he had promised to give her a lift to the airport. He did not want to see her go, had grown fond of her, and intended to see her again.

Another two calls from his father….

And another on from Andy Chandler. He simply said, "call me asshole," and hung up. Kidder tried to remember how many times he had been called an *asshole* lately, and then began wondering if he was one?

Then, after picking his poison, he was about to call the retired detective back when Kantz's phone call jolted his ear.

"If you don't have a body, I'm not interested."

"No, no body," Jimmy coughed into the phone, was dealing with a hangover, EP could tell. He could not blame him. "But I got something you're going to want to see. You should come down here as soon as you can. I don't want to ruin the surprise, but the search team found something in the swamp."

"All right," Kidder stretched and began walking back to his bedroom to take a shower. "Got to give me a couple of hours though. I got to get cleaned up, and then take Mahan to the airport. Bureau has reassigned her to another possible serial killer case in Boise, Idaho of all places."

"Lucky her…"

"Yeah," EP was about to hang up when he remembered Andy Chandler had phoned and decided to pry at Tuesday's mind. "Say Jimmy, do you remember Andy Chandler?"

"Sure, the scumbag of the department. He shouldn't have been allowed his pension if you ask me. Why do you ask?"

"Has he tried to contact you?"

"No."

"He hasn't tried to talk to you about Kinsinger, our investigation?"

"No. What's up Kidder? Want me to go knock on his door, crack his skull, and steal all his booze?" He laughed.

"No, but I think he knows something. Just a hunch. I'll keep you posted."

"Do that."

The conversation ended, and Kidder called Andy back while he stripped himself of his clothing and prepared to shower. He answered on the first ring. "Didn't think you were going to call me back sport?"

Kidder did not like being called *sport*. "What can I do for you Andy?"

"This isn't something that should be discussed on the phone, where are you?"

"At home."

"I'll be there in thirty minutes, wait for me!"

Andy Chandler abruptly ended the call, leaving no room for EP to stop him from coming over, but left him standing in the middle of his room, stark naked, and glaring at his bare frame in the dresser mirror. He decided it was time to trim his black locks of hair, his curls were getting out of control, and even decided to grow the patch of hair on his chin out more. It would look good, he thought, maybe make him seem tougher...like Brad Pitt.

He remembered he had company on the way and climbed into the hot water, and shaved everything but his chin.

Then, he put on another pot of coffee and waited for Andy Chandler.

While he waited, he wondered what Andy

wanted with him. Whatever it was, he knew it could not be good.

*

Kidder stopped by his father's office before picking up Mahan.

His talk with Andy Chandler had been brief.

His father was in, welcomed him inside his office. "You don't look so good," Stephen Kidder noticed, and directed EP to take a seat. "I'm sure you have plenty of vacation days lined up, you should take them. Maybe go somewhere? Your mother and I worry about you being such a homebody sometimes. Can't be good for you mentally."

"Shut up." EP did not know how else to say it, or know another way to get his father's attention. He had it now. "Andy Chandler just stopped by my house this morning dad, he told me some things, told me some things I was not expecting to hear."

"Andy Chandler is a disgrace to the department and a disgrace to this city. You of all people should know that. How dare you come into my office and tell me to *shut up!*"

"Shut up!" EP was not going to back down. "Is it true?"

"I don't know what you're talking about...."

"Did you give him the money?"

Stephen Kidder did not answer, but removed himself from behind his desk and walked over to the window, overlooking the city of St. Augustine. "I only did it to protect this family, to protect the *Kidder* name. You can sit there and look at me with accusing eyes if you want to, but one day you'll understand. One day you'll know what it's like to have to make tough decisions, and to deal with the consequences.

It's the world of politics son, nothing more. And it's in your blood whether you like it or not, and you'll be in my shoes one day. I don't expect you to understand right now, but you will. I promise you, you will."

"Shut the fuck up dad! You should have told me you knew about Abraham Kinsinger four years ago. You should have told me you assigned Andy Chandler to go behind my back, and whenever Abraham's name popped up as a possible suspect, you should have come to me..."

"It wasn't that simple son..."

"Explain that to me father, why wasn't it that simple? You had the name of a possible suspect, and you hid it from me. You could have pointed me in the right direction, but you didn't. Explain that to me."

"And you could have found Abraham Kinsinger yourself if you were good enough. Maybe then I would not have had to go behind your back."

"Fuck you!"

"No, fuck you!" Stephen Kidder was back at his desk now, his eyes dark with anger, his forehead wrinkled. "It was an election year, do you understand that? Just a year before that, Abraham Kinsinger and Miguel Hampton had done some remodeling work on some of our properties. Those properties, I might add, you will one day inherit. Do you know what would have happened if I went public with the information I had back then, what the headlines would have read?" He paused, he knew nothing he said would satisfy his son but he continued anyway. It was time to clear his chest. "I'll tell you, you ungrateful little shit. They would have said, *serial killer works on Kidder home, serial killer close to city leader!* And do you know what would have happened then, we would have lost everything, everything Ernest. Everything would have been lost, all that our family has worked for over the years and those properties you are going to one day inherit, and you know what would have happened to those? We would have lost them, had to sell. We would've been run out of this town, our legacy destroyed."

EP did not care, never cared about his last name. He was getting the truth, but not satisfied. "Did you tell Andy Chandler to destroy evidence?"

"Yes."

"Did you pay him?"

"Yes."

"Are you sure he destroyed everything?"

"No."

There was nothing more EP could do, was not even sure what he was going to do with the information he had. He was sure Andy would disappear for a while, until the money ran out, but was sure that he'd be back for more, with more threats. And he knew the only reason Andy had told him everything was so that his relationship with his father would deteriorate, to get him involved, incase he needed more leverage one day. But he would never be able to look his father in the eyes again, wanted nothing more to do with him.

He wondered if he would be able to keep the information a secret.

Then he turned to leave his father's office, but stopped at the door and turned back towards him. He pointed his finger at the man he had to call *dad,* wanted him to hear him loud and clear. "You have blood on your hands father. You have cost a lot of innocent people their lives. I hope you can live with that. And I hope you know what you're doing with Andy Chandler. He'll bury you if he has to. He's not someone you want to mess with."

"I'm not someone he wants to mess with."

"Blood is on your hands father, think about that. Just think about it, while you masturbate over our last fucking name."

"That's right!" His father called him back as he opened the door and prepared to leave. "It's *our* fucking last name. Your last name is Kidder too, incase you've forgotten. So go clean up son, the bathroom is right down the hall. Blood is all over your hands as well……"

*

Mahan knew something was wrong at the airport.

EP had kept mostly to himself the entire drive, said absolutely nothing during check-in, and sat slouched, staring at ground, outside the gate. "Want to talk about it?" she asked, wished him in better spirits, wished even more that he would have invited her over last night.

I still don't understand why he didn't.

"No, not really. Just be glad you're getting on that plane and getting far, far away from here. Wish I could join you," EP paused, climbed to his feet and hugged Mahan with a warm embrace as it was time for her to board her plane. "The FBI doing any hiring?" he added jokingly, squeezed her some more, pulled her close and rubbed her back. He'd always remember her back, he thought, as she read him like a book.

"Your father?"

"Something like that."

"Politics?"

"Something like that."

"I'll call you when I land, you can tell me about it," Mahan walked away from him, had been dreading this moment for the past couple of days. She had never had trouble saying "goodbye" before, but she just could not bring herself to do it.

She did not want to.

Wanted to kiss him, thought about it.

"Sounds good," EP called out to her. "I'll be at home, in the kitchen," knew what he was about to say would piss her off. "I'll be making crab claws, just how you like them, with a nice bottle of chardonnay...."

"You know what Kidder," she yelled from the gate, smiling, missing him already. "You really are an asshole!"

*

EP did not wait around to see the plane take off.

He was not the sentimental type, never had been, nor did he see the reason for it.

Dramatic airport goodbyes were for the movies anyway.

It was not that he did not have a heart, more so he just did not want anyone to see it.

Or maybe he did not want to feel it, the sadness.

Either way, he was back in his car before the plane took off.

And he was driving when his cell phone rang.

It was the reporter, Miranda Richardson.

"What can I do for you Miranda?"

"I heard Mahan was leaving tonight, is that true?" He could tell she was running her fingers through her fiery red hair and smacking on a piece of gum. "She gave me my exclusive today, hell of a story I must admit. I hope this isn't the last we see of her.

We had a lot in common you know…"
"I just saw her to her plane," EP knew what was coming next.
"Are you okay?"
"I'm fine Miranda."
"So," she paused, giggled, and continued smacking her gum. "So I guess that means you're free tonight?"
"Yes." Again, EP was not devoted to sentimental bullshit. "I am."

*

Five hours later, Mahan's plane landed in Boise, Idaho.
The weather was different, not as suffocating, and the air was thinner.
Her stomach growled as she thought about the Sunshine State.
And she started craving crab claws again!

EPILOGUE

Kidder could not believe his surprise.

Tuesday sat next to him as he read it....Abraham Kinsinger's diary.

That's what it was, a diary.

Motherfucker even wrote it in red ink!

It had taken two days for the crime lab to put all the words into place, the swamp won at first, many pages wet, smudged in wet soil, even a few smears of blood ran words together, Abraham's blood, they knew now.

The likelihood of Abraham surviving the gunshot wound was slim, if not impossible, but Kidder knew he would not be able to rest easy until his body was found, or a piece of it anyway.

He took a break before the last couple of pages, in need of more coffee.

But returned seconds later, and finished the diary of his first serial killer.

I am not retarded, slow, nor do I have a handicap flier dangling from my rearview mirror.

Have I made mistakes?

Sure, I should have never put those bodies in my car before I torched it. Trust me, I'll never forgive myself for that. If I had not done that, then not only would the piggies still be searching for them, but they'd still be searching for me as well, or trying to pin everything on me anyway.

Alas, one person's loss is another person's gain.

Tis the way of the world.

And I lost my composure, allowing the piggies to gain their evidence against me.

That's okay though, I'm still writing from this motel room, my next victim is sitting next to me on the bed and has no idea what's about to happen to him. What a fucking moron, really. I mean think about it, how in the hell can all these people I've killed never feel the presence of evil close by, staring them in the face? And this guy, on the bed, he has no idea I'm the one that took his daughter, no clue as to what I'm up to. I even told him my name was Angelo, do I look like a fucking Angelo? I'll say it again, loud and clear, MORON!

I swear, I could have told some of them what I intended to do before I did it, and they would have laughed, not believed me.

But they all believed me when death came.
And in the end, they all wanted to die.
I was too much for them.
Anyway, I don't know what's going to happen tonight, I'm excited, but wary nonetheless.
I have a plan, of course, but nothing ever works according to plan.
Nothing.
And if this doesn't workout, then maybe no one has to worry about me anymore……..
But if it does workout, by chance, maybe I'll write again.
Maybe I'll write another diary, elaborate just a little bit more about who I am, what I'm about, and what I'm going to do….
Ah, who am I kidding?
If I get the chance, I'll write another story.
I'll tell someone else everything, let them read my new diary.
Every serial killer has their thing, their niche, and this is mine.
It's what I do.

Until then, maybe I'll tell you goodnight, friend…………..
I did say maybe, right?

Sincerely,
Abraham Kinsinger.

Made in the USA
Lexington, KY
09 July 2012